The Columnist
and
The Conformist and the Misfit

The Columnist
and
The Conformist and the Misfit

Two Novellas

Mark Carp

Copyright © 2018 by Mark Carp.

ISBN: Softcover 978-1-9845-5910-4
eBook 978-1-9845-5909-8

All rights reserved. No part of this book may be reproduced or transmitted in any form or by any means, electronic or mechanical, including photocopying, recording, or by any information storage and retrieval system, without permission in writing from the copyright owner.

This is a work of fiction. Names, characters, places and incidents either are the product of the author's imagination or are used fictitiously, and any resemblance to any actual persons, living or dead, events, or locales is entirely coincidental.

Any people depicted in stock imagery provided by Getty Images are models, and such images are being used for illustrative purposes only.
Certain stock imagery © Getty Images.

Print information available on the last page.

Rev. date: 12/17/2019

To order additional copies of this book, contact:
Xlibris
1-888-795-4274
www.Xlibris.com
Orders@Xlibris.com
781990

The Columnist

By Mark Carp

The people must be free to decide and understand the meaning of freedom.

Mark Carp

Dedication

To Aunt Mildred Cornblatt, a nice lady

CHAPTER I

The Journey Begins

I realized I was living a myth. I had become another parrot, repeating the shibboleths of my brethren. I knew at that moment how wrong I had been. I had to get off the "reservation" and start thinking, analyzing.

I hovered over my keyboard and knew why. As I looked out of my office window, the evidence lay before me. Unemployed men and women filed into a building to see if they qualified for additional payments. Next to that building was a courthouse where lawyers argued over a test case that called into question the legality of raising the minimum wage in spite of unemployed people who lacked the skills to be hired at that level of compensation. Adjacent to that building were the legislative chambers where legislators debated over programs that would force the already-weak banking sector, in the name of social justice, into making loans to people who couldn't repay them.

Along the streets, picketers marched with placards that indicated the whole of society had to do more to help the ever-increasing total of downtrodden who lacked the basics the public schools had failed to give them.

Meanwhile, legislatures across the country were trying to pass legislation to make it harder for business to operate, no doubt exacerbating the social problems they professed to try and cure.

I was thinking of the noticeable mess and the fools and their followers, myself included, who got us here and I began to type. I condemned the intellectuals, the educators, the legislators, and their surrogates, who promised a better life with fallacious reasoning that ignored the relevance of markets, independent thinking, and the rule of reason, and replaced these with palpable lies and exaggerations, which were easy to expose, but we were too caught up in them to question their relevance.

I entitled the article "The Freedom Manifesto" by Simon Atlas. It called for a reliance on individuals to make their lives better, and not be dependent on the legislators, schools and intellectuals who insisted on defining reality on their terms and not what it was. I listed many examples and closed with this: "No rational individual, thinking alone, would support such measures. Only if these people were caught up in group think could they go along with such ignorance, which would positively lead to society's failure."

When the column appeared, I was castigated by my friends and colleagues as one who had betrayed the cause of societal advancement. My response was continually, "If something doesn't work, you can't continually do more of the same in the hope that it will make things better. You can't ignore the 'law of gravity' forever."

I followed up this column with more such diatribes, which challenged the status quo, and, as I did, I found myself further alienated from my friends and colleagues. After a year of writing my words of castigation and protest, my nationally syndicated column was being dropped by more and more newspapers and outlets. With only my column being carried by a few more papers, I decided to cease my writing. My final words were these: "Is there no room for reason, or must we go along with group think, no matter how detrimental the circumstances?"

As I finished my final column, I began reviewing my e-mails. One struck me as quite unique. It read: *Come to Paragon City. You must see, first hand, what they are doing and who is responsible.*

Cynthia Wolfe

As I drove to the train station, I saw workers tearing down the statue of an intellectual who advocated the independence of thought, liberty and the primacy of the individual. It was no longer his world.

I boarded the train, which was now run by a government agency called The Peoples Transportation. The train was slow and the car filthy. Whatever the government seemed to touch, it made worse in the name of making it more equitable. I went to the dining car, which had recently been closed. Then, I was directed to the rear of a passenger car where snacks were being served. I ordered a Danish pastry, which was stale from age, and coffee, which was served cold because it was unable to be heated properly. I decided not to eat or drink and would wait to arrive in Paragon City for nourishment.

When I arrived, Cynthia Wolfe met me as I left the train. She offered to help me with my luggage, but I told her I could handle what I had brought. Cynthia told me she had parked nearby and I followed her to the car, where I placed my luggage into the trunk.

"Where are you taking me?" I asked.

"We are going to Vista Park, which overlooks Edgecombview, a huge subdivision made up of working-class residents, housing that's been wonderfully maintained in spite of its age, and shops that cater to the residents' needs."

"So why are you taking me there?" I asked.

"Because the city planners want to destroy Edgecombview by having large parts of the area condemned, then running a series of superhighways through the area."

"Who is behind this initiative?"

"The Paragon City Planning Department."

"Who is in charge of the department?"

"Oliver Reed."

"How did he reach his position?"

"He sold himself as a visionary and fools let him rise."

CHAPTER II

Oliver Reed

As Cynthia and I drove towards Vista Park, she told me about Oliver Reed.

"He owned, wrote and edited a Marxist daily newspaper called *The Rise of the Worker*," Cynthia told me. "The publication failed and he was hugely in debt. He answered an ad from *The Light*, Paragon City's leading newspaper, which asked candidates to apply to head the Planning Department of Paragon City. He sold himself to our mayor, Herbert Chase, the City Council, and now heads the department."

"How did he do that?" I asked.

"He had a degree in City Planning from New Age University and worked in a number of urban planning departments from where he was eventually forced to leave."

"Why?"

"He would try to organize the department along his lines of thinking, which were often at odds with the prevailing philosophy. Eventually, he was cast out of jobs, which, because of employees' protections, were hard to be fired from.

"He went for an interview and soon picked up a sketch pad and began drawing a series of superhighways through Edgecombview, which would all but destroy the neighborhood."

"Is such a highway system needed?"

"Not at all."

"Then when did your mayor support his candidacy?"

"Because Reed sold himself as a planning visionary, and the unions would get most of the construction jobs so they fell in line and encouraged the mayor to support his candidacy."

"Was there anything else?"

"Yes, the mayor has two cohorts he depends on for their advice and counsel."

"Who are they?"

"There is Erskin Caldwell and Joseph Martin."

"What is their motivation to support Reed?"

"When the essence of Edgecombview is destroyed, swaths of housing can be picked up at bargain prices. These two already operate a real-estate rental business that is fronted by a lackey named Solomon Frazier. When Caldwell and Martin obtain the houses, they will rent them to the poor who will have housing subsidies approved by the Paragon City Public Housing Authority and City Council."

"So now you have planning, corruption, stupidity and wasteful spending being sold in the name of the public interest."

"Exactly."

"How long did it take Edgecombview to evolve to its present status as an area that fulfills the needs and expectations of its residents?"

"It's been developing for fifty years."

"Without strong planning, subsidies, etc?"

"Exactly."

"Now, only to be destroyed in literally a speck of time."

"It looks that way, Simon."

"And how are the media reacting to Mr. Reed and his plans?"

"What do you think?"

"They love grandiose ideas with hyperbolic catchwords that they believe represent societal evolution," I said.

"No matter how stupid!"

"The dumber the better. ... Who is supporting Oliver Reed besides the mayor, City Council, the unions and others who will benefit from the largesse he will try to spawn."

"The upper crust of society, many of whom are the idle rich. They see Reed as some kind of intellectual force who is remaking patterns of living."

I had dinner with Cynthia that evening at my hotel, the Organic Arms, where the rooms were small and the rates high. She told me of a meeting that society people were having tomorrow evening at the Pinter Gardens, a condominium, to hear Reed speak.

"How did you get invited?" I asked.

"My mother is hosting the party."

"So she supports Reed?"

"Of course."

"And you don't."

"As you have heard, emphatically no."

"I respect my mother, but I have nothing in common with her views. … You see, she and my father have been divorced since I was a child. He was quite a bit older than she when they married. My mother was young and beautiful when they wed and Daddy owned a number of coal mines, which he still does. His money gave her an entrance into the upper reaches of society, which she sought."

"How does your mother feel about his coal mines?"

"She would like to see them closed."

"Why?"

"Because the people she associates with would."

"Is that the only reason?"

"It's the only reason I can understand."

Cynthia and I went to Helene Wolfe's apartment to hear Oliver Reed speak. When we arrived, Cynthia greeted her mother coolly, though the two hugged. Hors d'oeuvres were being served by a maid who lived in Edgecombview. She was married to a carpenter.

We arrived ten minutes prior to Mr. Reed's talk. As I looked over the guests, I could sense there was great expectation by what appeared to be non-critical invitees.

At 8 P.M., the time of the scheduled talk, the guest speaker had not arrived. Helene Wolfe began to stir uneasily, wondering to an invitee, "I hope Mr. Reed didn't forget. ... I know he's such a busy man."

The guest nodded cordially.

At 8:10 P.M., Helene tried to reach Mr. Reed on his cell phone. There was no answer.

At 8:15 P.M., as the guests began to stir uneasily, Helene again tried to reach Reed on his cell phone. Again, there was no answer.

"It's obvious he forgot," one guest said.

"I bet he's on his way," Helene said. "He was probably delayed in a meeting. His time is so valuable." The guest demurred and waited, along with others, for Mr. Reed.

At 8:20 P.M., an irritated Helene Wolfe walked out into the hall and saw Oliver Reed, accompanied by an associate, amble towards her unit. He was a short bearded man who was overweight and wore thick glasses. Helene walked into her residence and told the guests, relieved, "He's coming."

The guests waited expectantly.

CHAPTER III

The Illusionist Speaks

Reed made his way to the podium and began to speak of his high-speed superhighway system that would go through Edgecombview, linking the outer-reaches of Paragon City with the downtown. He spoke of the time motorists would save and began to explain how expert planners could make great changes for the better in an urban world.

Following his talk, Reed received enthusiastic applause. Helene Wolfe approached the speaker and praised him warmly for his "wisdom and intelligence." Then she asked for questions. Cynthia Wolfe raised her hand and her mother called on her.

"Mr. Reed," she asked, "has anyone calculated the cost of the highways, the cost of uprooting the Edgecombview community, and whether this grandiose highway is really needed?"

Rather than answer the question, Reed began to talk of how brilliant planning efforts are going to remake the country.

After Reed finished his non-answer, Cynthia said, "These superhighways through Edgecombview are a physical and financial monstrosity. You, Sir, are an impostor and the people who follow you are fools."

Helene Wolfe was aghast at her daughter's comments and apologized to Reed.

Cynthia turned to me and said, "Let's leave these idol worshippers to their guru. I can see where this is headed."

Cynthia abruptly left, with me following, as an embarrassed Helene Wolfe apologized for her daughter's "rude outburst."

The following morning, I met Cynthia at a diner in Edgecombview where she and I spoke over coffee. Signs such as "Stop Reed" and "Don't Fix What Isn't Broken" began to appear in shop windows.

I said to Cynthia, "It looks like the people are trying to fight Reed and city government."

"They have a real struggle on their hands. They'll be opposed by editorial writers, machine-style politics, and 'experts' who think they're smarter than the people they're supposed to serve."

"Amen to that," I replied.

"Look," she said, "there is a lecture today at Newman College, given by Professor Herb Heartman, that I would like for you to attend with me."

"What's it on?"

"The logic of experts and why people are often unfit to make decisions that they feel are best for themselves."

"How interesting," I said sarcastically.

We left the coffee shop and drove some fifty miles in Cynthia's car to the campus where the lecture was being given.

On campus, we saw a bonfire and books being tossed into it.

"What's this about?" Cynthia asked one of the students.

"We're burning the literature of people whose philosophy is dangerous and out of touch with the times."

"Like whom?"

"Ayn Rand, Milton Friedman and Friedrich Hayek."

"What did they have in common?"

"They believed individuals are best able to make their own decisions, and individual liberty is the force that best moves society in a positive direction."

"And what do you think?"

"In a complex world, the individual can't be depended upon. He must grant to experts the right to decide for him."

"Shouldn't people have the right to choose?"

"No," the student said emphatically. "They will only waste time and resources."

We were aghast after we listened to the student and left the book burning.

Next we entered the lecture hall to listen to Professor Heartman.

The professor entered the lecture hall to enthusiastic applause. He walked to the podium and looked over the vast crowd. Then he began to speak.

"The days of the individual and individualism are doomed. Experts will plot the course of mankind and lead the people to utopia. The people must get behind the experts who will create a Super State and guide them. The people will follow because it's in their best interest to do so."

Those lines produced rousing applauses.

Heartman smiled and looked over the cheering, enthusiastic crowd.

Then he said, "It is the mission of Newman College to create the experts to lead us away from wasteful individualism to the promise of a better tomorrow through planning."

That line brought another rousing set of applause because the students were applauding themselves, the vanguard of the new order, the leaders to whom the people must relinquish their rights and power.

Following the talk, people who wished to ask questions were directed to a microphone in the rear of the auditorium.

Cynthia, as the second questioner, asked, "Suppose the experts to whom power is deferred are incorrect in their views. What recourse do the people have once they have agreed to give up their rights?"

Heartman answered: "The experts won't be wrong. They will have at their disposal the great minds of science, engineering and economics. It will be brilliant people consorting with other brilliant people, marching in lockstep to produce the glowing consensus that will lead society."

"Haven't 'experts' been wrong before?" Cynthia asked, following up.

The question brought jeers from the students and Heartman refused to answer.

Cynthia walked back to her chair. As she did, she was booed and pelted with debris. She sat, a bit unnerved, next to me. She said softly, "I guess dissent is dead."

The next questioner asked, "When do you think the majority of societal decisions will be in the hands of experts and not the people?"

"It should occur in the next decade," Heartman answered. Then he scanned the audience and said, "Students of Newman, it will be up to you to choose the best direction for the people. They will need you and depend upon you."

After hearing that answer, Cynthia turned to me and said, "Let's leave these educated idiots and their messiah. I've heard enough."

I nodded and Cynthia and I got up and went to her car.

As Cynthia and I drove to Paragon City, she said, "The art of critical thinking is dying. A certain class of people is being told how smart it is and the populace will depend on its members. If the people buy into this nonsense, society is headed for a fall."

I told Cynthia I agreed. Then I began asking her personal questions.

CHAPTER IV

<u>Getting Down to Brass Tacks</u>

I surmised Cynthia was about thirty years old. She was approximately 5'5" tall with long red hair and was extremely well built. I asked her if she was married. Cynthia told me she divorced two years ago, after being married to an attorney.

"How about you?" she asked.

"My wife died tragically in a car accident five years ago," I said.

"I'm sorry," Cynthia said softly.

"Do you have children?" Cynthia asked.

I shook my head, no.

"How about you?" I asked.

"No," Cynthia replied.

After more personal conversation, I invited Cynthia to have dinner with me at a restaurant of her choosing.

She told me her favorite place was Grantley's, an eatery with a vast menu, great service and excellent, uniquely prepared food.

"Cynthia, so far you've been right about a lot of things. I'll take your word for this."

She smiled adorably and I returned the smile.

As we sat in the restaurant, I said, "It's amazing to me how easily people can be led."

"Yes," Cynthia replied, "the more educated the people are, the more incapable they seem to be of critical thinking."

"History has demonstrated for us," I replied, "that more revolutions have been led by supposed intellectuals, who were supported by people but who made the people worse off."

"Start naming names."

"The Russian Revolution of 1917," I said, "and the Chinese Revolution of Mao Tse-tung, which occurred in 1949."

"History has had its share of sheep in wolves' clothing," Cynthia replied harshly.

"Yes," I verified, "so how about if we change the subject?"

"To what?" Cynthia asked.

"To you."

"I'm an open book," she said.

"Okay," I replied, "I'd like to begin reading."

"You're welcome to start."

"Are you seeing anyone now?" I asked.

"Not in the least."

"Why?"

"I've had some suitors, but haven't found the right one."

"Why do you think that is?"

"Perhaps because I'm too independent."

"I like independent women."

"And I'd like to think I like independent men," she said, smiling.

I returned my date's attractive smile.

"How old are you?" Cynthia asked.

"I'm Jack Benny's age," I said.

"Thirty nine eternally?"

"Only til I reach forty."

"And when will that be?"

"Some six months from now. And may I ask your age?"

"Guess."

"A hot twenty nine."

"You've got it."

"And when will you hit the big three oh?"

"About the same time you hit forty."

"I knew from the start we had something in common," I laughed.

"I like a man with a sense of humor."

"You need one in this cockamamy world," I chuckled.

We continued to talk on a variety of subjects through dinner: Economics, news, and the direction of a country that stressed relinquishing power to experts at the expense of individual liberty.

"You know," I said, "it's popular to demean the *Founding Generation* as slaveholders, misogynists, or whatever cliché fits a momentary narrative that doesn't conform to the facts."

"Yes," Cynthia said, "if you repeat a lie long enough, you end up with perversity masquerading as truth."

"But what the Founders gave us was a system with enough firewalls to keep the demagogues at bay."

"But eventually the demagogues find holes in the system, and distortion and ruination creep in," Cynthia replied.

"We're two people seemingly fighting a tidal wave."

"But we can have a voice."

"How?"

"You must begin writing again."

"My days as a mass-circulation columnist are over."

"So go to the underground."

"What are you talking about?"

"Start publishing on the Internet."

"What should I call the column?"

"How about: 'To Whom It May Concern'?"

"Let me think about this."

"I'll be glad to assist you with your writing."

I nodded and smiled.

CHAPTER V

"To Whom It May Concern"

I sat at my word processor, took Cynthia's advice, and began my column which I called "To Whom It May Concern."

I wrote: "Individualism and liberty are precious commodities, hard won, often after bloody struggles against tyrants and kings.

"If the individual gives up liberty for additional security, he will likely find when he chooses to reclaim liberty, he can't. Instead, he will face a jungle of regulations and laws, often administered by impersonal bureaucrats who are ignorant and duplicitous of the rules and regulations they are supposed to administer.

"But now the individual can't opt out. Instead, he has become a slave to the masters who were empowered to serve him.

"The individual will now find he's but a number, and his life is no longer his own."

Cynthia walked into the room as I typed and she read what I had written, which was now visible on the screen.

After she read the initial paragraphs, Cynthia said, "Keep going, you've become a valuable voice."

I nodded and continued to type.

I finished my column and posted it. After a few days, I began to receive e-mails that supported my position on individuality and liberty.

I decided I would post a column regularly. I would do so after studying an issue in depth and indicate what would be the better solution: Individualism or *Group Think*.

In the meantime, I needed to support myself, which would require advertisers to buy space next to my column. Cynthia began contacting firms to see if they would be interested. Typically, large firms, which were dependent on government revenue and prevailing public opinion, would not consider advertising with me. However, I began to receive interest from small firms, generally startups, which were owned by independent-minded entrepreneurs, unafraid to challenge the status quo. We were kindred spirits, believing in initiative and defying trends.

Eventually, I began to build a following, much to the consternation of those who had a vested interest in the ever-emerging status quo. However, people such as Oliver Reed, when asked to speak before civic groups, would rail against my position, indicating when decision-making is in the hands of experts, society would advance.

"The individual," he said, "must relinquish authority to experts, because we know what's best for the people."

When I read Mr. Reed's criticism of me, I wrote a column which began: "'Experts' can never admit when they're wrong. Generally, all they can do is advocate more of the same and perpetuate failure. And they have the nerve to condemn the people as ignorant."

CHAPTER VI

All Is Not Well in Edgecombview

"It's time the citizens of Edgecombview have their voices heard and elect me," Jack Trimble, a candidate for the City Council, told a large crowd which had gathered at the corner of Broadway and Fourth Street to hear him speak.

"If elected, it is my intention to stop Oliver Reed from destroying our community. It's time for the individual to stand up for what's right and not defer his independence to those who profess to know what's best for him.

"Elect me and I will fight for you and expose the corrupt consolidation of experts, politicians and bureaucrats. ... I'll work for what's proper and in your best interest."

The assembled applauded wildly, with the exception of Solomon Frazier, the lackey who ran the real estate company of Erskin Caldwell and Joseph Martin, two cohorts of Mayor Herbert Chase, whom he depended upon for advice and counsel.

The next day, Frazier met with Caldwell and Martin, telling them of Jack Trimble's apparent ground swell of support from the people of Edgecombview.

As the three sat in Caldwell's office, Frazier said, "The people of Edgecombview won't sit idly by and have their community wrecked by Oliver Reed's grandiose highway program. What are we to do?"

"We must throw our support behind the incumbent, Councilman Everett Slocum," Caldwell said.

"But the people know he's corrupt and won't support their interest," Frazier replied.

"We must stop Trimble," Martin concurred.

"But how?" Frazier asked.

"We'll mobilize the mayoral office, the media, the academics, and the uppercrust of society who believe in Reed's omniscience," Caldwell said.

"Like-minded fools flock together," Martin said. "So we should be able to fight and defeat Trimble."

As Cynthia Wolfe and Simon Atlas were having dinner together that evening, she said, "The people of Edgecombview will not be sheep led to the slaughter by the corrupt and foolish. They are throwing their support behind Jack Trimble. They will fight."

"But there is a lot to overcome," I replied.

"Yes, but they have a lot to fight for."

"But will that be enough?"

"We'll see, as we are about to witness a stark human drama," Cynthia said.

As I began my column that evening, I wrote: "History is full of examples when the few had to overcome the powerful. Only time will tell if they will succeed and what the ultimate outcome will be if they do.

"A society that believes in the freedom of the individual provides the best opportunity for advancement.

"But such a road is hard to travel and is fraught with many fissures along the way."

In my own way, I was a witness to the sanctity of my words because I would now be a spectator to see if Edgecombview could save itself from the vicious egotists, fools, frauds and corrupt who sought to destroy it in the name of societal advancement.

Yet Edgecombview was one battle in a country that was now beset by many confrontations between the rights of the individual and those who wanted to think for him or her in the name of what they considered to be progress.

I interrupted my musings by picking up the phone and calling Cynthia. I asked her if she wanted to attend a play with me.

"What's it called?" she asked.

"*Unmasked*," I said.

"What's it about?"

"How the Founders of the country had ulterior motives when the Constitution was adopted, and that their goal was merely self-enrichment."

"It might be good for a laugh," Cynthia said.

"It's not meant to be funny," I replied.

We attended the play, which was full of bromides and clichés, painting the Founders as exploiters who worked in their narrow interests and not the people's.

After the play ended, the audience yelled for the playwright to appear. Magnum Burns came on stage to rousing applause. At that moment, Cynthia and I turned our backs to the stage and left.

Outside of the theatre, Cynthia said to me, "Facts can be distorted and history rewritten to sway the people until they became acolytes of the current narrative."

"Yes," I said, "if you repeat lies long enough, black becomes white and down becomes up."

Cynthia and I walked a couple of blocks and came upon a charming little coffee shop called Defiantly Good.

"Let's stop here for some dessert and coffee," I said.

Cynthia nodded and we walked in. We were soon seated and waited on.

"What's the theme of your next column?" she asked.

"Evildoers can control the narrative and create an alternative universe that destroys, rather than enhances, civil society."

"What examples will you use?"

"Nazi Germany in the 1930s and 1940s."

At that moment, the owner came over and asked how we enjoyed our dessert and coffee.

"Delicious," I said, and Cynthia nodded in concurrence.

I said to the owner, "You look perplexed."

"I am," he said.

"Why?"

"I have a health department inspection tomorrow."

"So what's the big deal?"

"The health department has little regard for its rules and regulations. Things are done arbitrarily and on a whim. They can close you up and put you out of business."

"You'll be alright," I said.

"I'm not sure," the owner replied.

As we walked out of the coffee shop, Cynthia asked, "After speaking to the coffee shop owner, do you have any more ideas for columns?"

"Yes."

"Let me hear it."

"It's as Lord Acton said, 'Power tends to corrupt, and absolute power corrupts absolutely.'"

CHAPTER VII

The World We Know

Following the dessert and coffee we had at the restaurant where the owner feared an inspection and an arbitrary ruling from the health department, Cynthia invited me to her apartment. I could see the superior building had begun to decline.

I asked Cynthia, "Why isn't the apartment house being maintained as it should be?"

"Paragon City is considering a rent-control measure, and the owner has advised the tenants that until the matter is resolved where he has satisfactory control of the property's destiny, he won't be investing any more capital in it."

"So the legislature of Paragon City is considering being the judge and jury of how much landlords should charge and what tenants should pay."

"Yes."

"On what basis?"

"Only the council people know what's best."

"I always thought that if a landlord and tenant agreed to a price, that was how grown-ups did business."

"You're old fashioned," Cynthia quipped.

"I guess so," I replied.

"Enough of such talk," Cynthia said. "Let's be people."

Cynthia and I sat on a large sofa and she put on soft music and began to smile at me alluringly.

"Are you comfortable?" she asked.

I smiled.

She put her arms around my neck and drew my lips to hers. I then put my arms around her and we began to kiss passionately. As we did, I felt a unique sensation that was the result of a sensual union with a kindred spirit and a beautiful woman. We reveled in each other's arms. Then we made love, beautiful, exquisite love. We were now soulmates of mind and body.

As we awoke the next morning, we began to smile at one another.

"You're pretty good," Cynthia said.

"As a columnist," I joked.

"Yes, but also as someone I can share my bedroom with."

"You're something," I said.

"Only with someone I can be comfortable in giving my body to."

"And I love when I have your body."

Cynthia got up slowly, sensually, still seemingly reveling in the lovemaking we had.

"What are you going to do today?" she asked.

"Write."

"About what?"

"Our sensual union from last night."

"Do you think anyone would be interested?"

"In the world we live in, probably more so than the columns I write."

"Aren't you being a bit cynical?"

"Frankly, my dear, I don't think I'm being cynical enough."

"I guess sizzle sells."

"More so than philosophy."

"I was told we had *left the caves*."

"You're listening to the wrong people," I said mockingly.

"And whom should I listen to?"

"Perhaps only listen to the empirical evidence in your soul," I replied.

"I guess that's why we're together."

"Are you saying our empirical observations are the same?"

"We were drawn together because we see the world alike," Cynthia said.

"In spite of how we've been told to think."

"There are always two views: What you're told and what you observe."

"In other words, Cynthia, experience is your best and truest guide."

"In the end, Simon, we inevitably educate ourselves to the best course of action."

CHAPTER VIII

The Corruption of Power

Professor Herb Heartman's new book, *The Inevitability of Experts,* had become a national best seller. As a result, he was asked to address the graduating class of Newman College. Following his speech to the attentive graduates who envisioned themselves as the new order of experts who would lead society, he awarded the valedictorian prize to Augustus Sinclair.

Following the ceremony, he met with the tall, sandy-haired, reed-thin, bespectacled Augustus and told him a rare opportunity awaited him.

"What's that, Sir?" Augustus asked expectantly.

"You have the opportunity to work in the Planning Department of Paragon City for the great urban visionary Oliver Reed."

"Uh, I'm overwhelmed … when do I start?"

"Eight o'clock Monday morning."

"And Mr. Reed is expecting me?"

"Yes. I've told him about your academic record and brilliance as a student."

"Thank you, Sir," Sinclair said, overwhelmed.

Sinclair met Reed at the appointed time and asked what responsibilities he would be assigned. Reed was noncommittal but told him to review past reports from the Planning Department. Reed then laid a stack of old reports on Sinclair's desk and told him to review them.

"I'll await your comments," Reed said.

Sinclair began reviewing the reports with great relish, writing extensive comments about their content.

After two weeks, he gave his comments to Reed who thanked him.

"When will I hear your response?" Sinclair asked Reed.

"Soon," he replied.

"I have a lot of big ideas for the Department, which I would like to discuss with you," Sinclair said enthusiastically.

"Put them in a report for me to review," Reed said nonchalantly.

Sinclair nodded vigorously and began writing his report.

Two weeks later, he handed Reed the report.

"Here you are, Sir," Sinclair said, as he gave Reed the one-hundred page report.

"When will we discuss what I have written?"

Reed smiled and said, "Uh, when I get to it."

Sinclair, a bit taken aback, then asked, "What other assignments do you have for me?"

"I'll let you know," Reed responded.

"What should I do in the meantime?"

Reed walked away and Sinclair sat at his desk, waiting for directions. After two weeks of idleness, Sinclair knocked on Reed's office door.

"Come in," Reed said.

Sinclair walked in and Reed told him to have a seat. As he sat, he asked Reed, "Have you reviewed my comments on the past reports from the Planning Department or my ideas for the Department?"

"Not yet," Reed said.

"Why is that?" Sinclair asked hesitantly.

"Uh, I've been busy with other matters."

As Sinclair stared at Reed's empty desk, he said timidly, "Uh, when do you think you'll review these matters?"

"Sometime soon."

"Could you please be more definite?"

"Look, my young friend, you don't seem to understand reality."

"I don't know what you mean."

"It is my goal to achieve absolute power for the Department, so we are the complete masters in planning matters. We must be in a position when no one can question our powers or decisions. In life you can either rule or be ruled, and it's my intention to rule completely and unabashedly."

"How about the people you are serving?" Sinclair asked timidly.

"The people must be made to follow, either out of fear or because of brainwashing."

"But there will be dissenters," Augustus interrupted. "They always are."

"Lenin, it is believed, coined the phrase 'Useful Idiots' and we will have enough of them to carry the day."

"Your plans are very ambitious, but I recall the phrase, 'You can fool some of the people some of the time, but you can't fool all of the people all of the time.'"

"My young friend, whose side are you on?"

"I'm on your side, but there are limitations to everything."

"When you rule, there can be no limitations. Your power must be absolute."

"I see."

"Now please leave, I'm a very busy man."

Augustus stood up, a bit shaken, looked at Reed's empty desk, and left, badly disillusioned.

He decided to leave the office and walk. As he did, Augustus questioned the premise of the education he had received. In large measure, he felt duped and sensed he had become nothing more than a fool with a diploma.

He soon decided to send an e-mail to Simon Atlas. It read: "I need to see you."

CHAPTER IX

Reality Seeps In

Simon met Augustus Sinclair at Defiantly Good, the coffee shop he and Cynthia went to after they saw *Unmasked*. Simon saw the owner and quipped, "I see you're still open, so I assume you survived the inspection by the Health Department."

"Kind of."

"What do you mean?"

"The Department wants me to make modifications to the restaurant on the basis of consumer protection."

"Are such changes needed?"

"No."

"But I assume you'll have to make them."

"It's either that or close up. ... You know I'm at the mercy of bureaucrats who interpret the rules and regulations as they see fit, not necessarily what they are."

"Can you afford to make the changes?"

"Not really."

"What are you going to do?"

"I may close up and tell my employees that because of the Health Department, I can no longer operate profitably."

I looked at Augustus who was seemingly absorbing every word of our conversation, perhaps getting the education he never received at Newman College.

The owner walked away and Sinclair stared into space. Then he said, "When reality is ugly, it hits you in the face like a sledgehammer."

I nodded.

"You know," he said, "there are a lot of grasping, ignorant people in the world of public policy who work in the interest of themselves, not the people's."

"Go on," I said.

"But it's hard for the people to fight back once they've ceded power to government. Then government is the ruler, not the servant."

"So," I asked, "what is the value of what you've learned at Newman College?"

"It's got the value of the paper my diploma is printed on, not much more."

"So in a short time you've begun to see things for what they are, not what you were educated that they were."

"It appears that way."

"So what's your next step?"

"I'm going to leave Oliver Reed's Planning Department in Paragon City and look for productive work elsewhere."

"Good luck," I said.

"Say, would you need some help with your column? Uh, I have strong writing skills."

"If I hired you, I couldn't pay you much."

"But at least if I were with you, I could do something productive and write factual content, without being at the mercy of a crazed egotist."

"Then I'll pay you what I can."

"I'll be pleased to work for you."

A day later, Sinclair and I met with Cynthia Wolfe for breakfast at Defiantly Good.

I told her that Augustus would be joining me to help write my column. I asked her if we had any more advertisers so we would have additional monies enough to pay him.

She said, "Quite likely, a few more advertisers should be on board soon."

"Good," I replied. "So when the extra money comes in, I'll give it to Augustus so he can support himself."

At that moment, the owner of Defiantly Good came over and asked us how we enjoyed breakfast.

I told him "very much."

"How about you?" I asked Cynthia and Sinclair.

"Delicious," they said.

"How are things?" I asked the owner.

"Not very well."

"Why?"

"As a result of the recent Health Department inspection and what it would cost me to comply with what I'm told I would have to spend, I've decided to close."

I turned to Sinclair and said, "Now you're getting the education you thought you had."

Sinclair pursed his lips and smiled cynically.

CHAPTER X

By Any Means Necessary?

Sinclair and I coauthored the next column entitled "The Cost of Misinformation." Under our byline, we wrote: "It's hard to admit when you're wrong, especially when you've heard for years how enlightened you've become because of your education and sundry associations.

"But you must grasp the truth and face reality. Sometimes accepting the truth is hard, but it is a necessity for the individual and society if each is to progress.

"Perhaps it's hardest to accept the truth when the forces of society are arrayed with you. Conformity can impose its own malevolent effects.

"But someone or something has to restrain the forces of evil or else society will perish."

Sinclair and I discussed our opening paragraphs and agreed that is what we wanted to say and how we wished to say it.

We soon finished the column and decided to meet Jack Trimble, the City Council candidate who was running for the seat in Edgecombview.

"How are things coming with the campaign?" I asked him.

"My support is strong with the people, but I'm worried there can be a substantial number of illegal votes that could sway the election. You know if I'm elected that could well mean that the nefarious plans of Oliver Reed, Erskin Caldwell and Joseph Martin are defeated."

"But they will not take your election lying down. They will fight you every step of the way," I said.

"If that is to occur, we must summon all the forces we can to meet the challenge," Trimble replied.

"The battle will be tough, but the fight will be joined," Augustus said.

Trimble smiled and I said, "My young friend seems to be learning on the job."

"That's the best education we can get," Trimble said.

I concurred, "That's the education that's most worthwhile."

"You know," Trimble said, "people like Oliver Reed feel they are so enlightened, they feel tampering with the vote is justified because their mission is so noble."

"You always worry in a society of laws," I said, "that what's legal won't be enforced because, as they say, 'Who's watching the watchers'?"

"You mean," said Sinclair, "forces can become so powerful the law and what is legal literally become impotent."

"Precisely," I said.

"I suppose at some point," said Sinclair, "you must look to the judges to arbitrate justice."

"The trouble with judges," Trimble replied, "is they become slaves to their ideology, and not servants of the law."

"So, you're saying," said Sinclair, "society can rot from internal machinations as well as an uninformed and naïve electorate."

"Precisely," Trimble said.

"Throughout history there have been examples of both," I replied.

"So what is the immediate answer for the people of Edgecombview as they face the threats they do?" Sinclair asked.

"We must beat back the forces that seek to destroy the community," Trimble replied.

"By any means necessary?" Sinclair queried.

"I don't want to lower myself to the clandestine activities of my opponents," Trimble said.

"But what if it becomes necessary?" I asked.

"I want my community to survive," Trimble said, "but the more legitimate my course of action, I'd like to think, the better off everyone would be."

After that comment, the meeting ended.

CHAPTER XI

The "Genius" Destroys

With city government, members of academia, the media and the uppercrust of society largely behind him, Oliver Reed went on a speaking tour to further cement support for his grandiose highway plan that would destroy the essence of Edgecombview.

Speaking before a coalition of civic groups which favored the plan, Reed claimed the effort would not only create efficiencies in transportation, but would demonstrate the wisdom of the "genius of expert planners."

Following his talk, he invited questions. Augustus Sinclair, his former employee in the Planning Department and now the co-author of my column *To Whom It May Concern*, asked, "Mr. Reed, in addition to the huge costs of the project, has anyone considered the human toll on the residents of Edgecombview?"

Reed answered dismissively, "For society to advance, it is sometimes necessary to break a few eggs."

Sinclair responded, "Suppose it were your eggs that were broken and you had no recourse to fight back?"

"My young friend, I work for the good of mankind, I'm their benefactor."

"Contrary to what you think, you're not everyone's benefactor."

Rather than engage Augustus in a discussion of philosophy, Reed turned to an armed guard and nodded. The guard approached Augustus and began to escort him from the building. At the back door, Augustus yelled, "A resort to thuggery means your position can't stand up to simple inquiry."

After Augustus was removed from the building, Reed went on extolling the virtues of his plan.

The following day, Augustus and I coauthored a column entitled "Failure to Listen." In it we wrote, "Those who feel they have a monopoly on wisdom will soon find their wisdom is nonexistent. Wisdom can best be perpetuated by listening more and speaking less. To ignore this simple fact, is to perpetuate ignorance at the expense of intellectual growth."

Jack Trimble won the race for the City Council seat with a plank of opposing Reed's highway plan. As a member of the Council, he began to muster support to deny Reed the funding for his plan. Ultimately, however, because of the behind-the-scenes efforts of Erskin Caldwell and Joseph Martin, the plan was approved. However, because of the largesse of the plan, substantial funds would have to be obtained from the federal government to complete the funding so the massive project could begin.

As a result, Reed, Caldwell and Martin went to the nation's capital to begin lobbying legislators in their behalf.

Some in Congress were skeptical of Reed because of the power he would be given with their assistance, and his belief that experts are best suited to decide the fate of the people, which many in Congress saw as a usurpation of their power. As the vote neared, Reed, Martin and Caldwell knew they were one vote short of passage, so they went to Senator Peter J. Flagg whose son was a struggling architect. After the three exchanged pleasantries, Caldwell said, "If you give us your vote and the funding is approved, there may be a position for your son on the project's architectural team."

Senator Flagg thought for a moment and said, "For me to give my vote for the project, my son, Peter J. Flagg, Jr., must be the project's chief architect."

At that instant, Caldwell's and Martin's eyes turned toward Reed who said unhesitantly, "The job is his."

"How about President Consenti," Caldwell asked, "do you think he might veto the legislation?"

"No," Senator Flagg said, "anytime a large spending plan needs approval, he will sign it into law. He loves grandiose policies and spending programs to which his name will be forever linked."

With the funding approved, soon armies of bulldozers and workers were approaching Edgecombview to begin destroying the vibrant community. As they did, the unions applauded the initiative because of the opportunity for self-enrichment. A prominent commentator applauded Reed's "genius and awareness, hoping it could be the dawn of the new normal!"

After considering these responses, the next column I coauthored with Augustus Sinclair began, "Have the victims of genius ever been polled as to what they think of the masters of their fate?

"If they would be, the likelihood is there would be far fewer geniuses.

"In the main, genius, apparently, is now available on the cheap."

CHAPTER XII

The Nature of Things

As the demolition of Edgecombview began, homeowners who would be spared demolition began to panic, putting their homes up for sale en masse.

At a meeting of a civic group, when a spokesman from Paragon City urged the residents to stay and not panic, Louise Fletcher, a longtime resident, rose and spoke, "Why don't you buy my home and live next to the expressways? If you think it's such a good idea, I'll trade my house for your home."

She was followed by another spokesman, Paul Williams, who said, "We're sick of people who use the legislative process not to serve us, but to try and control our lives. We're slowly losing our rights to those who profess to have superior intelligence and know what's best for us. These people must be stopped."

Williams' comments produced rousing and sustained applause.

Next, one speaker after another rose to lash out at the highway project, which was now proceeding.

As Erskin Caldwell and Joseph Martin met, Caldwell said to Martin, "The panic selling has begun. Houses are now available at prices that were half of what they were six months ago. Start sending

Solomon Frazier out to acquire them and start having legislation prepared to get housing subsidies for those to whom we will rent the units."

Legislation was soon prepared, and supported by advocates of Affordable Housing. Among its staunchest supporters was Helene Wolfe, Cynthia Wolfe's mother, who had begun dating Oliver Reed. These two were often photographed dining at restaurants and these pictures were frequently published in the society page of the *Paragon Times*, the city's highest-circulation newspaper.

Helene Wolfe organized a speakers' bureau to advocate for Reed's views and subsidies for affordable housing at Edgecombview.

Ms. Wolfe's activities were detailed in the *Paragon Times*, where she was often pictured talking to civic groups in support of affordable-housing legislation.

As Erskin Caldwell and Joseph Martin read of Ms. Wolfe's initiatives, they laughed out loud.

"You would think she's on our payroll," Martin said to Caldwell. "We couldn't have a better advocate."

As Cynthia Wolfe and I were dining together, her mother's advocacy of Oliver Reed was discussed.

"Critical thinking has been replaced by imagery that is ignorance masquerading as brilliance," Cynthia said.

"Not a great way to achieve gains in public policy," I replied.

"Perhaps another column awaits," she suggested.

"Undoubtedly so," I affirmed.

I sat at my word processor without my co-author, Augustus Sinclair, and thought about composing on the lack of critical thinking when deciding important issues. However, I couldn't concentrate. I began thinking of Cynthia Wolfe, her beauty and intellect. I called her and she asked how the latest column was coming.

"I'm having trouble concentrating," I said.

"That's not like you, Simon," Cynthia replied.

"I know, besides Augustus isn't here."

"What's the problem?"

"I have other things on my mind."

"Like what?"

"Like you."

"Well, you can do something about that."

"Okay, beautiful, what should I do?"

"How about a nice dinner."

"Then what?"

"Simon, we'll let nature take its course."

I came to Cynthia's unit and said, "You're looking more lovely than ever."

She smiled at me alluringly.

"Where to?" I asked.

"How about Lutèce, a quaint little French restaurant?"

"That's quite romantic."

"That's what I have in mind," she said.

After a night of dining with Cynthia, I drove her to her apartment.

"Would you like to spend the night with me?" she asked.

"That's something that won't require any legislative act," I quipped.

"No, it's a shared impulse for two people who are united in heart, mind and spirit."

"I couldn't have said it any better."

Then we rode up to her apartment in an elevator, as we stared into each other's eyes.

CHAPTER XIII

The "Inequality" of Legislation

As Erskin Caldwell and Joseph Martin began to accumulate houses at fire-sale prices and legislation was about to pass to give them housing subsidies, Caldwell said to Martin, "We need an amendment attached to the bill we've had introduced in our behalf."

"What for?" Martin asked.

"These units must be free of future rent control."

"How can we get that done?"

"Go to a councilman and have him introduce the amendment along with some superfluous amendments. The council people never read the legislation anyway."

"Whom should we get?"

"Contact Gary Franks."

"Why?"

"He's easy to buy and sell."

"Suppose he objects."

"We'll make him a partner by giving him a small piece of our deal. That should seal matters."

Franks was soon contacted by Solomon Frazier and told to meet him at the front of a decrepit dock area in Paragon City. There,

Frazier gave him the clause that would eliminate the houses from future rent control, along with some superfluous amendments.

"What's in it for me?" Franks asked, after he read what was given him.

At that moment, Frazier handed him a brown bag with ten thousand dollars of cash inside.

Franks felt the bag and asked, "How much is in here?"

"Ten Thousand Dollars."

"I'll let you know."

"I'll keep the money until you decide."

"I'll give you my answer tomorrow at 8 P.M., right here."

"Okay," Frazier said.

Franks met Frazier at the appointed time and said, "Keep your bag of cash."

"I kind of thought we had a deal," Frazier said.

"Look, with the money Caldwell and Martin are going to make at Edgecombview because of the abolition of future but inevitable rent control, there should be more for me."

"How much are you looking for, Sport?"

"The ten thousand dollars, plus I get three percent of the deal as a limited partner."

"Let me talk to Caldwell and Martin."

"When will I have your answer?"

"I should have it for you two days from now."

"Okay, we'll meet here then at the same time."

Frazier nodded and left.

That evening, Frazier met with Caldwell and Martin and told him of Frank's counteroffer.

"That thief," said Caldwell, pounding his fist on the table. "Whom does he think he's dealing with?"

"Calm down," Martin said. "Give the whore his three percent. We'll own the little bastard, and if we need more favors, we'll continue to have our go-to guy."

"But can we control him?"

"If we can't, he may find himself the victim of an accidental drowning. … We've gotten rid of people before."

"Okay, Solomon, close the deal," Caldwell said, now calmer.

Within weeks, Councilman Franks introduced a series of amendments to the house-subsidy bill which included the one that would free Edgecombview from any future rent control.

After a ceremony at City Hall, Mayor Herbert Chase signed the legislation into law, calling it "a great day for civic progress." He was unaware that Edgecombview would be free of future rent control. Then the Mayor called on Oliver Reed to speak.

Reed ambled to the podium and said, "This day will long be remembered for its communalism and progress as the forces of planning, the legislature and the people have been united in the cause of progress in Paragon City."

As Augustus Sinclair and I listened to Reed speak, Sinclair said, "Tyrants have used the law in the name of progress to destroy the people."

"Yes," I said, "at one time they even praised Mussolini."

"Why?"

"Because he claimed to have made the trains run on time."

"I suppose we have grist for a column."

"Let's go to it, my young friend."

As we sat at the word processor, I began to type, "When the legislature acts to favor some in the name of all, there will inevitably be problems. No citizen should be more equal than another."

CHAPTER XIV

Chicanery at the Polls

As time passed, and Erskin Caldwell and Joseph Martin worried about Oliver Reed accumulating too much power in Paragon City, possibly to their detriment, they felt it would be in their interest if he would represent the state as a Senator. They decided to meet with the party chiefs and sound them out on a Reed candidacy. After hearing of Reed's possible candidacy, the party chiefs were noncommittal.

Following the meeting, Caldwell and Martin met with Reed and his significant other, Helene Wolfe, to discuss a run for the Senate, emphasizing that that could lead to him becoming President of the country, where he could help implement a program of Total Expert Rule. Reed was supportive of the plan as was Helene, who envisioned herself as the First Lady.

After hearing Reed's initial reaction, Caldwell and Martin decided to plant the idea of a Reed candidacy for the Senate with some local political clubs which believed in the planning he advocated.

Soon, Reed began speaking before such groups and galvanized their support. Next, these groups began to combine for a "Draft Reed For Senate Run." They did so by rallies and marches where Reed would appear late in the event and speak of his qualifications and visions.

Eventually, Reed was nominated and ran for the Senate, though the pundits felt he had little chance of winning because of a lack of support in the state's rural counties. When Caldwell and Martin saw the initial polls that Reed was behind in the rural counties, they began to meet with leaders of these subdivisions to sway support for their candidate. Soon it was arranged for bundles of cash to be transported to these counties where the monies would be distributed during pro-Reed rallies, with the hint that more would be available on election day and buses would be used to transport the voters to the polls.

With their plans in place immediately prior to the election, Caldwell and Martin met to devise a plan to destroy enough votes of Reed's opponent, the long-serving incumbent, P. J. Fairman.

The night of the election, Caldwell and Martin waited anxiously for the returns to come in.

"Do you think we did enough to get the fat bastard out of the State?" Martin asked Caldwell.

"If things go according to plan, Reed should win," Caldwell responded.

"The trouble is these are plans and there are results, and sometimes the two are miles apart."

"I think we have enough apparatus in place to get our man elected."

When the votes were counted, Reed was elected by one-hundred and fifty votes, with unprecedented support coming from the rural counties, where Senator Fairman, the pollsters indicated, was still the people's choice.

Immediately, Fairman's supporters cried foul and demanded a recount. However, the vote was certified and Reed was on his way to the nation's capital to represent the state as a Senator.

After the election, I sat at my word processor with Augustus Sinclair and wrote, "With the election of Oliver Reed to the Senate, the people may have spoken but their words have disappeared."

Augustus read my opening sentence and said, "Nothing else needs to be said."

I smiled, but continued to type.

CHAPTER XV

The Thankful Good-bye

"I'm glad we got Oliver Reed out of town," Caldwell said to Martin.

"Yes, I think Lord Acton was right when he said, 'Power tends to corrupt, and absolute power corrupts absolutely.'"

"He should have said," Caldwell mentioned to Martin, "it's better to rule than be ruled."

"Isn't that the truth!" Martin replied.

As the two continued to talk, Helene Wolfe and Oliver Reed readied to leave Paragon City. However, the night before the couple was to move, Reed was feted at City Hall with a dinner in his honor.

Outside of City Hall, former residents of Edgecombview marched with placards which said, "Let's hope Oliver Reed doesn't do to the country what he did to Edgecombview."

When one of the protestors was asked by a member of the media, "What is the meaning of your protest?" He responded, saying, "You have two eyes, remove your 'ideological blinders' and think for a change instead of parroting what you believe your editor and paper think is fashionable."

When the reporter was about to ask a follow-up question, the protestor ignored him and kept marching.

Inside the building, Reed was honored like a conquering hero. Words of praise rang out from the various dignitaries who praised Reed's "vision" and "work for the benefit of his fellow man."

When Caldwell and Martin heard those words of praise, they faced each other and laughed.

Finally, Reed was to deliver the evening's keynote speech. He got up and ambled to the microphone to a standing ovation. He took off his glasses and wiped them carefully. Then he put his spectacles back on. He carefully surveyed the audience. Then he began to speak.

"Ladies and gentlemen of Paragon City, it has been my pleasure to serve you. Now, thanks to you, I have an opportunity to represent our state and nation on the most-important stage of all, the country's capital.

"There, I will try to implement my and the people's vision of a richer tomorrow through better planning."

At that moment, as if on cue, Cynthia Wolfe rose and began to applaud. She was followed by those in attendance who gave Reed a three-minute standing ovation, which would have lasted longer had Reed not motioned the attendees to sit so he could conclude his remarks.

As those present sat, Caldwell said to Martin, "I now know Shakespeare had it right when he said, 'All the world's a stage, and all the men and women merely players.'"

"Even Shakespeare wouldn't believe this comedy," Martin quipped.

"But let's look at it this way," Caldwell countered, "we're having the last laugh."

Then Martin smiled and Caldwell returned his smile, as Reed continued to talk.

The following day, Reed and Helene Wolfe left for the airport to begin their new life in the nation's capital.

As they did, I began to draft a column with Augustus Sinclair present. I wrote, "If the planner is given power without strictures, he can destroy what civilization has built because his folly remains unchecked, and the people he is supposed to serve become his servant, fearful of the planner's every move. Because the people understand, perhaps more than their elected officials, what untapped power means, they will not sit idly by and have their lives ruined.

"Eventually, the people will revolt, whether by force or at the polls, and they will move to take control of their own lives.

"They will establish a means of doing so which will be based on freedom of choice, not a dictatorship manned by those who are supposed to know what's best for him or her."

As Augustus read what I had written, he said, "You needn't say any more."

"Why?"

"Because everyone who understands will know what you mean."

"And how about those who don't?" I responded.

"Some people never learn," Augustus said.

"Nonetheless, I have more to say."

"Remember, Shakespeare said, 'Brevity is the soul of wit.'"

"Shakespeare didn't know Oliver Reed."

"No, but I'm sure he was familiar with those who were just as bad."

I decided to stop typing and told Augustus he should finish the column I had started, tomorrow.

Augustus said he would return tomorrow at 9 A.M., and said, "I don't think you need a coauthor on this one, you're totally on the proper course."

I smiled and Augustus left. Then, I picked up the phone and called Cynthia Wolfe. She asked what I was doing. I told her of the column I was writing and began to read it to her.

"As usual, you're on the right track."

"I'd like to 'track' over and see you this evening."

"Your wish is granted, Mr. Atlas."

CHAPTER XVI

My Lover and My Work

As Cynthia and I dined in her apartment, she said, "I really liked what you started to write in your column. It has such a ring of truth."

"Thank you," I replied.

"Following dinner," Cynthia asked, "what would you like to do?"

"How about if we take a nice long walk, arm and arm, and just be people, away from the problems of the day?"

"That's an idea that's as good at what you're writing in your current column."

Following dinner, she and I left her apartment and we began to walk, holding hands.

"It's nice to stroll leisurely with the man I love," Cynthia said.

"I feel the same," I replied.

Then I stopped, put my arms around her, and kissed her as passionately as I ever had.

"I love when we have these moments together," Cynthia said, "when we're two lovers, being ourselves, away from the slings and arrows of outrageous fortune."

"The problem," I replied, "is that the slings and arrows of outrageous fortune always seem to find us, no matter where or when."

"So what's your solution?"

"We can still be ourselves, in spite of everything," I said. "When I'm with you, I feel a sense of wonder, as if the problems of the world had disappeared."

"If life were only so simple," she sighed.

Then we continued to walk in silence, our pace leisurely, and I could think of nothing but Cynthia: Her looks, her intellect, her spirit. I gently turned her and headed back to her apartment. She understood the gesture, and followed my lead. We entered her unit, and I lifted her up, cradling her in my arms, and then as I carried her into her bedroom, she smiled at me winsomely. I then laid her gently on the bed, and I began to undress her. She reveled in the gesture. Cynthia then lay completely nude as I stood, taking off my clothes. As I did, she held out her arms, beckoning me to join her, beckoning me to make love to her. As I joined Cynthia in her bed, our lust was uncontrollable, and our feverish lovemaking was nothing like I had ever experienced. As we completed our orgasm, we continued to hold each other, each smiling uncontrollably at the other.

"This has been some night," I said.

"I happen to agree with you," she replied.

"It's funny how we seem to seldom disagree," I laughed.

"Ah," Cynthia said, "if life were only as simple as we have just seemed to have made it."

"Life will never be simple. We can only live as we see fit, be honest with ourselves and everyone else, and do what we think is best."

"Yes, but will we be eaten alive in the process?" she asked.

"We must confront life and be unafraid of the consequences of our actions."

"But will we be eventually overwhelmed?" Cynthia asked.

"Only time will tell," I said. "Remember, we can be scared, but we mustn't be afraid."

Cynthia began to contemplate the meaning of my words. Then, after a long pause, she asked, "Are you going to finish your column tomorrow?"

"Maybe I'll let my words stand as they are, without any more additions."

"That may be a good idea."

I replied, "I think we're a good idea."

Then my lover smiled at me and I returned her beautiful smile.

I came to my office early the next morning and reread the column I was working on. I knew at that moment it needed no more embellishment. Then, I put it on the Internet.

CHAPTER XVII

Is Magic Enough?

Oliver Reed soon began to gain support in the Senate from his colleagues, who marveled at his ability to gain power in Paragon City so as to rise from obscurity and ascend to the national political stage.

He could be a spellbinding, influential speaker who could draw people to him, because Reed was able to seize power and his fellow senators wanted to be in the vanguard of the authority he had achieved on the way to national office.

Soon after he became a senator, he was urged to address the elected body on gaining power. He ambled to the lectern and addressed his fellow senators. He said, "To achieve power, you must use slogans that are easily rememberable, that support your position, and the people believe are directions that will help them. Such slogans can be, a 'Square Deal,' a 'Fair Deal,' a 'Deal to Empower People,' etc. Then, regardless of how the people perceive the slogan, start to have agencies voted into power with specific functions, staffed by 'experts' whom we can control and appoint. Point out that these agencies will be administered by functionaries who are the best minds in their field, even if that's not the case.

"Most of the people, in my experience, will defer their rights to them.

"Now we control the agencies that control the people, all in the name of helping humanity.

"It's a simple blueprint, not at all difficult, in my experience, to execute.

"So join me, my fellow senators, and we can consolidate the powers we don't have and rule together, as if we're Kings." Many of the senators stood and cheered their new guru. Others, however, left the chamber in disgust.

Senator Urban Raymoon said to Senator Cass Sunman, after hearing Reed's speech, "We're here to do the people's work, not to enchain them in the name of doing their bidding."

"With the egotists and the frauds we have in this body," Senator Sunman replied, "Reed will become to a lot of members the new messiah. ... Many of them campaign one way, and as soon as they enter our body, they forget everything they've told the voters."

"Yes," countered Raymoon, "Reed can be the excuse for more legislative amnesia."

"No doubt, Senator Raymoon."

As Reed's address began to leak out, I sat with Augustus Sinclair and entitled our new column, "When Will the People Say Enough's Enough?"

I told Augustus to write the opening.

He sat at the word processor and began: "When freedom is gone, it's often too late.

"At that moment, when the people realize their predicament, they will revolt.

"Some revolts have been at the polls and have been peaceful, others have been bloodbaths.

"Ultimately, the people will reap what they sow."

"Read my opening," Augustus told me.

I smiled as I did and said, "Keep going."

He returned the smile and continued.

"To quote an often-repeated paraphrase of a Benjamin Franklin writing, 'Those who trade security for liberty deserve neither.'"

I read Augustus's last sentence and said, "History has often shown that the people will eventually realize the folly of their ways."

"Yes," Augustus said, "but it takes a lot of doing to eliminate their undoing."

Then I continued the column.

"In life," I wrote, "it's important to see legislators for who they are, not what you wish them to be. Elected officials are not magicians and every charlatan has a trick that will eventually be exposed."

I reread the paragraph I wrote and felt I had to say no more. Augustus read it and said, "Shakespeare had it right, 'Brevity is the soul of wit.'"

Then we posted the column.

CHAPTER XVIII

Reed, the Man for the People

Urged on by Oliver Reed, the Senate began to pass a spate of legislation that was never intended by the country's constitution. Quickly, the legislation to create new agencies was signed into law by President Frank Fairless, who feared Reed's growing influence and would not buck the country's rising star. Often these new agencies, which began to dominate even more of the country's activities, were staffed by egotists who had no real-world experience, but sought to accrue power through rule-making and edicts. Such rules mandated that every building permit that was to be issued, no matter how minor, had to be accepted or rejected based on its perceived environmental impact; the retirement ages for workers; expanded rights of the government to seize private property; and limitations of the rights of employers to deal with employees who refuse to do their assigned tasks. This rule-making had the further effect of dampening the already-weak economy. As the economy continued to weaken, a Draft Oliver Reed for President Movement began to emerge. As it did, Senator Urban Raymoon said to Senator Cass Sunman, "Now they want Oliver Reed, one of the architects of the folly, to lead the country."

"It's the old story," Senator Sunman replied, "if it doesn't work, do more of the same."

"If it weren't so sad, I could laugh," said Senator Raymoon.

"They say we're supposed to be the best and the brightest. ... There's quite a difference between reputation and reality."

"How right you are, Senator Sunman."

"Only he can save us," became the slogan as the campaign to nominate Reed as the party's presidential candidate grew in intensity.

The media, taken by Reed's supposed intellect, and in spite of the fact that his initiatives continued to wreak havoc on the economy, were nearly unanimous in their advocacy of his candidacy.

Members of the media, almost to a person, fell in love with Reed's grandiose command-and-control advocacy of unelected agencies controlling the lives of the populace because they thought the people were unfit to think for themselves.

An editorial in the *Gotham Times*, acknowledged as the country's newspaper of record, read: "The world has become so complex, we must look to the people who have superior intelligence to lead us. It is only by doing so that society will continue to advance and travel on the road to an unimaginable summit. Reed, clearly, is the man for the *times*."

As Cynthia Wolfe, Simon Atas and I were eating dinner together in Cynthia's apartment, she pulled out a copy of the editorial and asked us if we had read it. Augustus and I nodded solemnly.

"What is your opinion?" Cynthia asked.

"Since the *Gotham Times* is such an advocate of Reed, I guess the editorial writers on the paper won't mind if he is given the power to censor what they write," I said.

"Knowing how inane some of the editorialists are, they would probably welcome Reed's words from on high," Cynthia said sarcastically.

"That is," I replied, "until they see the light."

"Those kind," Augustus said, "would sooner have Reed dig their graves rather than admit they were wrong in the advocacy of that buffoon."

"It sounds to me," Cynthia replied, "you two have grist for another column."

I smiled and so did Augustus.

The next day, Augustus and I sat at the word processor, and I began to type.

I entitled the column: "Is It Better to Think Or Worship?"

I wrote: "If we give unthinking allegiance to fools, whom we wish to perceive as having wisdom they don't possess, we are on our way to perdition.

"Ignorant people is the foolish ruler's most-powerful tool."

As Augustus read my opening words, he said, "Your words are full of wisdom."

"But what impact will they have?" I asked.

"Eventually, they must."

"But what condition will society be in when they do?"

"We must," said Augustus, "have faith and keep doing what we're doing."

Then I continued typing.

CHAPTER XIX

My Reaction to Unfolding Events

Oliver Reed, with the help of party regulars and Helene Wolfe, his significant other, threw himself into the campaign to be nominated as his party's presidential candidate.

After meeting with party regulars, they agreed on dubbing him "The Messiah of the Future."

With the media behind him and some of the big-city bosses who thought they could achieve extra benefits by delivering votes to him, Reed went on a whirlwind campaign: Visiting cities and talking directly to the people, addressing organizations, and delivering TV speeches.

He said, "My visions would lead to *Utopia*, and if the people put their faith in me, they will achieve happiness."

As he said these words, paid stooges in the live audience leapt to their feet and the balance of the audience followed.

"The best is yet to come," he said, "the road to utopia awaits."

As Reed's campaign progressed, Erskin Caldwell and Joseph Martin assessed the situation.

"I think Reed will get the nomination," Martin said to Caldwell.

"Good," replied Caldwell, "the farther he's away from Paragon City, the more we'll control things and benefit."

"You know the promises he makes to the people will only increase their suffering."

"Of course, but we're the ones who have benefited at the people's expense," Caldwell concluded.

* * *

As Reed's campaign progressed, the media began to take greater notice of Helene Wolfe. They noted her sense of fashion and grace. Journalists began to emphasize her commitment to the campaign, her advocacy of the positions Reed espoused, and her belief that the great planning efforts will deliver relief to the people. The attractive Ms. Wolfe was often photographed separately from Reed as stories emphasized her striking looks and manners.

As Reed's campaign progressed, Cynthia Wolfe and I began to walk regularly in Summit Park, which overlooked Edgecombview, the community Reed's highway program was destroying.

"You know things are bad enough," Cynthia said. "Now it is possible that a grotesque fool will lead the country."

"Will this be the final nail in the coffin?" I asked.

"Eventually, the people will wake up."

"But will it be too late?" I replied.

Then Cynthia and I continued to walk, arm and arm, as we contemplated current events and an uncertain future.

After I finished my walk with Cynthia, I called Augustus Sinclair whom I was unable to reach. I returned home and began to compose a new column, which I entitled "Hope and Reality."

I wrote: "If the people cannot see what leaders, whom they've placed their faith in are doing to them, they're destined for a life of servitude and poverty, in the name of perpetuating the public good.

"The individual must develop critical thinking skills and fully analyze situations for what they are, not what they've been told they'll be.

"Critical thinking skills can only come with experience, knowledge and the ability to analyze events in their entirety, without picking those that seem to be beneficial, while ignoring those that don't.

"Remember the world is filled with wolves in sheep's clothing and the devil can take a pleasing shape."

At that moment, I stopped typing and read what I had written. Then I called Cynthia and read it to her.

She said, "Your words are profound and need no explanation. ... Maybe you should read them to my mother, Helene, as she campaigns with that grotesque fool."

"Some people," I replied, "only see what they wish to see; they don't see things for what they are."

"Life, when you act like that," Cynthia said, "is great until it's too late."

Then I filed my column.

CHAPTER XX

The Future?

As Oliver Reed's campaign for the presidential nomination progressed, it became apparent that he was going to be the party's standard-bearer.

"What do you think his chances are in the presidential election?" Erskin Caldwell asked Joseph Martin.

"Reed may be the man for the times. After all, so much of politics is based on hucksterism. Candidates are sold the way cars are. Nobody looks under the 'hood' to see reality. Appearance is everything."

"Maybe the people are ready to wake up."

"I wouldn't bet on it," replied Martin.

Reed won his party's nomination, and at the convention, he gave his acceptance speech.

"I'm honored to represent you in these times of challenge. But we'll meet the challenges together through better planning for the future. The Road to Utopia starts here, and it's up to the voters to join me on my journey. If elected, I will deliver a better life for everyone."

As Cynthia Wolfe, Augustus Sinclair and I listened to Reed's speech, Cynthia said, "Why can't people see through that grotesque fool?"

"Because he promises Heaven on Earth to his followers," Augustus said.

"If the people want Heaven on Earth, they would do well to look elsewhere," I replied.

"But apparently they're not ready for that," Augustus said.

I nodded in agreement.

In the general election, Reed faced Lucius Freedman, who advocated limited government, with decision making to be returned to the people, away from the tentacles of legislators and bureaucrats, away from the rule of the "enlightened" few. Because Freedman's position was alien to the *Gotham Times*, the nation's paper of record, the editor-in-chief, Fred Nettlesome, sought to tie Lucius Freedman to a scandal. As a result, he met with Joseph Sharpman, his top investigative reporter.

"We need Reed to win," Nettlesome told Sharpman. "Find some dirt on Freedman that we can taint him with, and do a series that continually reinforces his 'unscrupulous' character."

"Yes, Sir," Sluethman said. "I'll get right on it."

A month later, Sharpman met Nettlesome. "What have you found?" the editor-in-chief asked his investigative reporter.

"The guy is clean," Sharpman said. "He's like a Boy Scout."

"What kind of investigative reporter are you who can't find dirt on a politician? They're all corrupt."

"Honestly, Mr. Nettlesome, my staff and I have been digging for a month and Freedman is untouchable."

"I'm beginning to worry," Nettlesome said, "the polls seem to be narrowing. ... We must do everything we can to elect Reed."

"Do more pro-Reed editorials," Sharpman replied.

"Getting dirt on a candidate is among the means I choose to pursue now. That's what motivates a lot of people."

"I see you don't have much faith in the electorate."

"It's up to us to tell the electorate what it should know."

"What happened to truth?"

"Truth is what we say it is."

"Maybe at some point the people will reject what you're spoon-feeding them."

"Not on my watch, Mr. Sharpman."

"Don't be so sure," the investigative reporter replied.

As the campaign continued, the *Gotham Times* continued to pour out more pro-Reed editorials, citing his "intellect, wisdom and foresight" and his "ability to see the future."

"He is," another editorial noted, "the Messiah of Necessary Central Planning."

As election day approached, I wrote, with Augustus Sinclair at my side, "The voters must see things for what they are, not what they've been told they are. The road to Hell is often paved by blind allegiance at the expense of critical thinking.

"Once fools and foolish things are in place, one has to live with their consequences because they are hard to remove.

"It's up to the people to decide what their future is and who will receive their allegiance.

"May they make the right choice. The future is up to them."

As Augustus read my words, he said, "I would end it there."

CHAPTER XXI

Prelude to the Voters "Deciding" for Themselves

The campaign for the presidency was vicious, and in Oliver Reed's case unpardonable exaggerations about the few having the wisdom to plan for the many became the theme of the day.

Whereas Lucius Freedman electioneered on the primacy of the individual deciding the fate for himself and his family, Reed's theme was: "The Rule of Brilliant Planners is the Means to Future Tranquility."

In a televised debate that was marked by hissing and booing from paid protestors every time Freedman made a point, Reed closed with: "If you elect me, your future will be in the hands of the enlightened few who will care for the many!"

That comment was followed by Freedman who said: "What will the many do if they've given up their rights to the few who are corrupt, foolish and only concerned with themselves, at the expense of the many?"

In the deafening silence that followed Freedman's comment, Augustus Sinclair turned to me and Cynthia Wolfe, as we three watched the debate, and said, "Even paid malcontents realized the gravity of what Freedman said."

"I suppose," I said, "every 'dirty dollar' has its limitations."

"Yes," Cynthia said, "but I don't think the election will turn on Freedman's comment, profound as it was."

After an awkward silence, Augustus said, "You have to start somewhere."

"I'm afraid," I said, "the die has been cast, Reed can't be overcome."

"Stranger things have happened," Augustus replied.

Cynthia and I nodded in agreement.

The campaign continued as before, with Reed promising "tranquility to come from a brilliant elite" and Freedman expressing wariness "of such a problematic notion."

Then the polls began to narrow as Freedman's warnings seemed to resonate with the voters.

Meanwhile, as the polls narrowed, Fred Nettlesome, editor of the *Gotham Times*, met with his editorial writers. He told them: "I want more editorials written that support Oliver Reed. He's our man who must lead the nation and think for the people who are incapable of thinking for themselves."

"We'll continue to follow your wishes," said Jasper Toady, the lead editorial writer.

"However," said Samantha Eversharp, an assistant editorial writer, "why do you have such contempt for the people?"

"Because only when the smartest people lead by controlling the masses will society advance," Nettlesome replied.

"It may be that the people you think are brilliant may not be and the masses have more wisdom than you give them credit for."

"I know what I'm talking about, Ms. Eversharp."

"Is there room for deviation in our editorial policy," Samantha replied, "or must we follow in lockstep?"

"You're a fine writer, Ms. Eversharp; however, there are talented people who would take your place in a heartbeat."

"I was told when I was hired there would be latitude of thought and the ability to express one freely, without editorial constraints."

"Ms. Eversharp, your employment depends on what you write. Please decide if you wish to stay or leave."

Then there was eerie silence. Soon after, Samantha Eversharp turned in her resignation and the editorial staff turned out more pro-Reed editorials, much to the delight of Nettlesome.

CHAPTER XXII

The Results Are In

As Election Day approached, the big-city machines, on the assumption they would be ceded more power with an Oliver Reed victory, worked to get out the vote for their man.

Editorial writers, also from large metropolitan areas, churned out more pro-Reed editorials, on the basis the people were too ignorant to think for themselves.

In Paragon City, Joseph Martin and Erskin Caldwell worked on an elaborate plan to have voters, even if they weren't registered, bused to the polls, where they would be given money to vote for Reed.

Nationally, the other Reed stakeholders worked feverishly to have him elected.

As the polls narrowed, the pro-Reed forces heightened their efforts on behalf of their candidate.

As Augustus Sinclair, Cynthia Wolfe and I discussed the narrowing polls, Augustus said, "It looks like the race is coming down to the People versus the Special Interests."

"It's only those people who can think for themselves and haven't been brainwashed," I said.

"Yes," said Cynthia, "but are there enough thoughtful people to make a difference?"

"We'll soon see," I replied.

As Election Day neared, polls varied in their predictions. Some saw it as a race that was too close to call. Others predicted an easy victory for Reed.

Augustus and I sat at the word processor and began to brainstorm why the polls varied widely. We came up with these points:

(1) "Who is being polled and at what time?"

(2) "How are the questioned asked? Are they tinged in a partisan manner to direct a particular response?

(3) "Is the information received by the pollsters being interpreted promptly and properly?

(4) "Is there a suitable distribution of age, race, sex, geography and income levels in the sample?

(5) "Are the people sampled likely to vote?"

Then I said to Augustus, "Are the media cherrypicking the results they wish the people to hear, or are they reporting the poll results honestly?"

"You can trust the media as much as you can believe Oliver Reed," Augustus replied to my question.

I smiled. Then we began to compose our next column. We called it: "A Critical Look at Polling."

We concluded with this: "Think for yourselves and don't be guided by poll results."

The day of the presidential election dawned and Oliver Reed and Helene Wolfe were photographed as they entered their polling place to vote. They were accompanied by a huge entourage that included show-business personalities, society sophisticates, big-city bosses, and some business leaders who were promised government contracts for supporting Reed if he were to be elected.

On the other hand, Lucius Freedman was photographed alone as he entered his polling place to vote. His solo entrance seemed to symbolize a campaign that he was waging for individualism against insipid group think.

That evening, I, along with Augustus and Cynthia, watched as the poll results came in. In the rural areas, Freedman's expected strength exceeded expectations. He was also doing better in the suburbs. However, the substantial urban vote went decidedly for Reed in greater numbers than had been predicted.

As the result of the urban vote became clear, Augustus asked, "I wonder how much of the urban vote is a result of vote fraud?"

I replied, "I feel it's substantial because there is tremendous interest in having him elected, and those who can benefit greatly will stoop to nothing to bring about his victory."

At 3 A.M. the results of the election were announced: Reed had won narrowly, primarily as a result of the urban vote.

The following day, Augustus and I sat composing a column that reflected our instincts concerning the election.

We wrote: "What happened to one man one vote, or have we become unthinking coalitions that must vote as a brainwashed block? What is happening to independent thought and discourse? What is happening to Enlightment thinking? Is it to be discarded like yesterday's trash? We must not worship at the hem of the garment of people running for office. Alternatively, we must look beneath their facades and peer into their souls. We must examine their rhetoric, inside and out. We must ask: Do their past actions comport with their current promises?

"This is the responsibility of the citizen, and only by doing this is it possible to maintain freedom and independence in a civil society."

CHAPTER XXIII

The Reed Agenda

Oliver Reed addressed the country after his narrow election win. As he did, the newly elected president laid out his agenda: "With the help of the Congress, I will nationalize all remaining private enterprises in order to bring down prices and eliminate outrageous salaries to the malefactors of wealth. I will deliver utopia and take from those who live off the labor of others. The less fortunate will rise and the greedy will suffer."

Within days of his speech, Congress was presented with bills to nationalize all remaining for-profit enterprises.

Immediately, the President was advised that many big-business leaders who supported Reed expected relief from the nationalization bill, and sought to shower congressmen and senators with "contributions" so their companies would be exempted from such legislation. Soon, thousands of amendments were introduced and the nationalization bill died in committee. Many voters were outraged.

At a press conference, Reed was asked what he planned to do as a result of his legislative defeat.

"I will seize the remaining free enterprises through eminent domain," he announced. "I won't be deterred."

As several captains of industries listened to the press conference, Phillip Jones, president of Amalgamated Industries, said, "The fat son-of-a-bitch takes himself seriously. We'll have to make sure he understands the facts of life and who is to be favored and who is to be punished."

"Yes," echoed Louis George. "We helped put the fool in office and we have the ability to show him the door."

Moments later, Jones called President Reed's chief of staff: "Have Mr. President come visit me at my office. We have serious matters to discuss."

A week later, President Reed, accompanied by the Secret Service, was ushered into the office of Phillip Jones, who was flanked by several titans of industry.

"Sit down, Mr. President," Jones told him.

President Reed, as ordered, took a seat.

"Listen, Mr. President," Jones told him, "if you want to nationalize a few minor industries or institutionalize price controls on them, you have our blessing. But you're going to leave us alone, do you understand?"

Reed squirmed in his chair, but didn't say a thing.

"Well, Mr. President, what's your answer?"

"Gentlemen," he replied, "I must confer with my Cabinet."

"Don't you understand, President Reed, we are your Cabinet!"

"But I have constituents who elected me because of my campaign promises and a large part of the media who will hold me accountable."

"So if the remaining industries are nationalized and fools like you are put in charge, the already-weak economy will weaken further. More production will lapse, and there will be greater unemployment. What do inexperienced bureaucrats know about running complicated industries?"

"They will learn for the benefit of the people."

"You fool, they will act in their own self-interest and create more problems than already exist."

President Reed was speechless. "Governing isn't so easy," he thought to himself. His musings were soon interrupted when Jones barked, "We expect to see you back here in a week with your answer."

President Reed got up to leave and as he walked to the door, accompanied by his entourage of Secret Service personnel, Jones screamed, "One week, Mr. President."

But Reed didn't return. Instead he went on a whirlwind speaking tour promoting his nationalization agenda. As he did, many non-nationalized industries, fearing the future even more, stopped whatever hiring and investing they were doing, weakening the economy still further.

As Augustus Sinclair, Cynthia Wolfe and I watched these events unfold, we discussed the matter over dinner in my apartment.

"It looks like the road to utopia is perforated with potholes," said Augustus.

"Yes, and the people will suffer more at the hands of charlatans who will be egged on by the fools in the media," I said.

"I suppose," said Cynthia, "it's time for another column."

"Yes," I said, "the road to utopia has a remarkable amount of chasms."

"Indeed," Cynthia said, matter-of-factly.

CHAPTER XXIV

Will There Be a Day of Reckoning?

In view of Oliver Reed being at loggerheads with captains of industry over nationalizing remaining free enterprises, Cynthia, I and Augustus sat around my word processor.

I began to type: "A fool's paradise starts with the anticipation that a magic wand is in the hands of those who claim to be enlightened.

"By prestidigitation, he can make problems disappear that dullards like him have created initially.

"It's time an educated electorate understands the meaning of individual freedom and free enterprise, and not entrust their lives to people who have no sense of reality and what works best.

"It's easy to destroy and then hide behind slogans that you're doing the people's work. It's much harder to pursue profit and build something that the populace will find valuable.

"It's far simpler to loot and falsely parade your quarry in front of the masses. It's much more difficult to provide the real needs of the people they are content to pay for."

As Augustus and Cynthia read my opening words, she said they're "beautiful" and they're "also quite profound."

I soon finished my column and posted it.

Meanwhile, Oliver Reed continued his speeches to nationalize remaining industries, and the economy suffered as a result.

I picked up Cynthia at her apartment and we began to walk around Edgecombview, the original site of Reed's nefarious activities.

"Will the majority ever see things for what they are," I asked, "instead of being spoon-fed tripe from duplicitous people?"

Cynthia shrugged and we continued to walk in silence, thinking of Reed and the fool's paradise he helped spawn.

Meanwhile, as we walked through Edgecombview, we saw swaths of housing that had been cleared to make way for Reed's grandiose highway program that hadn't started, and heard of the immense profits that Joseph Martin and Erskin Caldwell had made by picking up housing cheaply as the long-term residents fled.

Meanwhile, it was uncertain when the highway construction would start and there was the possibility it would never begin because of the lack of available funds due to the lackluster economy.

As I looked around, I said to Cynthia, "It's easy to anticipate how grandiose programs and methods of governing can work. However, reality strikes when the final results and costs are tallied and the promised benefits are far from expectation."

"Yes," Cynthia said, "there is a great chasm between hope and reality."

"And I anticipate that gulf to widen with charlatans like Reed in power."

"Eventually," replied Cynthia, "it's up to the people to reclaim the sovereignty and not entrust their lives to those who claim to know best."

"How right you are, Beautiful," I said, smiling.

"But when will that day occur?" an unsmiling Cynthia replied.

I didn't answer and we continued to walk in silence.

CHAPTER XXV

They're After Me

I opened my mail and saw a letter from the Tax and Revenue Service. It read: "Your previous tax return has been audited and it appears gross miscalculations have been found. Please come to our office listed above and bring your tax returns for the previous three years."

I called Cynthia and read her the letter. She said, "They're after you and they want to put you in jail. They want you silenced."

"I realize that," I said.

"What are you going to do?"

"I'll bring them the tax returns and then I'll go into hiding."

"Why?"

"Because I don't have a chance."

"How about the column?"

"I'll continue it while I'm on the lam."

"That's very brave of you."

"I'm only trying to do what's right. ... You only live once, and I'm going to make the most of it. I'm no one's lackey."

"I know you're not."

A week later, I met with a representative of the tax service and handed him the requested materials.

"What's the best way for us to stay in touch with you?"

I gave the representative my address and left his presence.

I called Cynthia and told her to meet me in my apartment.

She was there when I arrived. Cynthia helped me pack and before I left, we embraced lovingly.

"When will I see you again, Darling?" she asked.

"When the people come to their senses?" I replied scornfully.

"That may be never," she said sadly.

"Have faith, Darling, we'll always be together in spirit, and you'll be at my side before you know it."

"How can you be optimistic at a time like this?"

"Because I sense the tide is changing," I said, feigning a sense of optimism.

We then had a long good-bye kiss.

"I'll see you soon," I said, displaying a feeling of hope I lacked.

Cynthia came to my apartment window with tears in her eyes. I looked up and she waved. I returned her wave, got in my car and left. Then I began to cry.

I began to drive through a country I no longer understood. I asked myself: "Am I in a nation that no longer understands human values, but defers to misanthropes and their slogans? Am I in a country where the populace has lost the ability to think and act rationally? Am I among the people who will willingly give up their rights on a whim?" As I mulled over these questions, I thought about the state of things and suddenly felt better. "The people aren't fools," I thought to myself. "They will take back their country either at the polls or by force. Sometimes, when things seem hopeless, it's actually the time for the greatest optimism. It's just hard to see and feel but it's there. I know it's there. It must be there."

I posted these sentiments in my first column, written on the run. While I knew, in reality, I was a fugitive from justice, I was determined not to be silenced. The government could hunt me, but it could not suppress me. Also, whether I was a lone voice, or a voice among the many who stayed silent, I would not be deterred.

CHAPTER XXVI

Life on the Run

I came to Fathom City, a metropolis in an adjoining state. As I entered the locale, I saw, amid the shuttered businesses, signs announcing: "A Teach-in On Liberty Tonight At 8 P.M. In Paine Auditorium."

I sat in the rear, not wanting to bring the slightest bit of attention to myself. Professor Horace Thoreau came upon the stage as a large audience eagerly awaited his presence. He stood behind the podium and said, "Liberty is hard won, often after a bloody conflict, but easily given up by accepting a doctrine that the people are incapable of rational thought and prudent decision making. Therefore, it's in the populace's best interest to give up their rights to experts and leaders who can decide for them.

"But in reality, whose interests do the experts represent, yours, the dispossessed, or theirs, the powerful who seek to maintain their hold at all cost, no matter what harm they cause?

"All you have to do is look around and see that what I'm suggesting is manifestly true."

Professor Thoreau continued his lecture for some twenty minutes and then took questions from the audience.

The first questioner asked, "Professor Thoreau, what you say is true, but how can we respond?"

"The people," Thoreau answered, "need to take back their liberty peacefully or through violence. I advocate a peaceful means of resistance and results that can be achieved at the polls. But sometimes desperate times call for desperate measures."

Another member of the audience said, "But President Reed has the Army. It would be easy for him to suppress a revolt."

"Frankly," the professor said, "I know many in the military are dissatisfied with President Reed, whose policy of disarmament has made our armed forces incapable of defending the nation."

"But do you think the military would side with a new regime that would force President Reed out of office?" the same person asked, following up.

"I believe," the professor replied, "the military would adhere to civilian control of our armed forces. All it is looking for is able leadership from above."

Another questioner asked, "What do you see in the not-too-distant future?"

"I foresee change. The people are too smart to be led by frauds in high places. At some point, they will realize they must be governed by those who understand the practical limits of government."

"Do you have a timetable in mind?"

"Only that the people's time will come."

The moderator then thanked Professor Thoreau for his presentation. I made my way to the podium where Professor Thoreau chatted with the moderator. After Thoreau and the moderator finished talking, I introduced myself to the professor.

"No introduction needed," said Professor Thoreau. "The tall, dark-complected muscularly framed Simon Atlas, who is a fugitive from justice, can be recognized anywhere. Your picture is now famous because the government is after you for writing the truth."

"At least we *understand* the truth," I replied.

"Well, Mr. Atlas, what is your next move?"

"I intend to keep moving and writing."

"Noble ambitions," the professor said.

I began to enter other cities where similar dissatisfaction mounted. However, I knew the major media, which supported Reed, would never understand the grassroots movement that was mounting and would not report on it. They had a vested interest in President Reed's policies, despite the continued failures these would likely spawn.

I soon called Cynthia Wolfe and told her what I was seeing.

"I know, Darling," she replied, "I read your last column."

I smiled and said, "I know you did."

CHAPTER XXVII

Finding the Truth?

I entered city after city and knew the Reed Administration was destined for a fall because his continued policies of Rule by an Expert Elite continued to bring destruction and desolation to the people. As Reed's popularity was plummeting, he decided to convene a meeting of his Cabinet. At the meeting, Agnes Triumpho, Secretary of Life, suggested that "in view of the difficulties we face, we can adopt a strategy that will buy us time until our planning efforts prove fruitful and win the people over."

"What are you suggesting?" asked Louis Summit, head of the Department of Optimism.

"A Charm Offensive."

"What are you talking about?" countered Summit.

"We can have prominent women address the nation and softly suggest patience for our policies is the best prescription for a bright future."

"Who would you suggest do that?" said President Reed.

"I think for the first address," said Ms. Triumpho, "we can have your significant other, Helene Wolfe, speak to the country."

"She can project a certain sense of dignity and stateliness at the podium," interrupted Summit.

"Plus, she's an attractive woman," chimed Sidney Voyeur, head of the Department of Knowledge.

It was unanimously agreed by members of the Cabinet that Ms. Wolfe should address the nation. A speech was written that indicated the masses must be patient with the Administration because utopia awaits. The speech highlighted certain accomplishments of the Administration that were implausible exaggerations.

The evening of the speech, some picketers marched outside of the studio demanding Reed resign and new elections be held. Other protestors marched with placards that stated: "Helene Wolfe Advocated An End To Coal. We Advocate An End To Nonsense. Reed Must Go."

The media, in general, reported her speech was exceptional in its advocacy of President Reed and his "intelligent policies." No mention was made of the considerable protests outside of the studio or general discontent in the country.

When Samuel Credible, a reporter for the *Gotham Times*, protested to his editor, "We're not giving the people the facts."

He was told, "The people are incapable of understanding what's good for them. It's up to us to 'educate' the masses."

"The people," Credible protested, "are smarter than you think. ... Maybe it is you, Sir, who is the myopic one."

"Mr. Credible," the editor shot back, "we must censor what is not good for the people to know."

"Are we a news organization or a propaganda wing for President Reed and his policies?"

"Mr. Credible, I'm a busy man with important duties and responsibilities. I really don't have time for small talk."

Before Credible could comment, a brick, with a note attached, shattered the editor's glass window and landed at his feet. The editor picked up the brick and read the note which said: "The people's best weapon is the truth. Start reporting it."

"The rabble doesn't understand what we advocate is best for them," said the editor.

"Maybe," said Credible, "it's the people who see the light and it's you, Sir, who's in the dark."

Credible left the office in despair, wondering if there was room for truth at his newspaper. He said to himself, "We censor facts and promote propaganda, not a great way to run an organization that's supposed to be in the news business."

CHAPTER XXVIII

Oblivious to Reality?

I knew the elites, many in the media, and numerous self-serving politicians were oblivious to the discontent sweeping the country. It seems most in high places thought only they knew what was best and were immune to the cause of people seeking freedom from the yoke of government.

The elites only mingled with themselves. They had become a closed society. But, I knew, when you close the windows and the sunshine can't get in, there can be a withering on the inside.

As a result, when societies fracture, the results can be ugly because the people could only be pushed so far. Suppression of natural instincts can lead to an explosion, and these aren't pretty. I continued to see the discontent rising in city after city and town after town.

I regularly spoke to Cynthia Wolfe about the unmistakable trends I saw.

She admonished, "Be careful, you're still a fugitive."

"I will, Darling."

"I need to see you soon, My Love."

"I think it might be sooner rather than later."

"Why are you so optimistic?"

"Because things are about to change, and I think for the better."

"Still, you must be careful."

After an eerie silence during which Cynthia seemed to be gathering her thoughts, she said, "I continue to read your columns and find they're more penetrating than ever. You've become the voice of truth, the voice of the people."

"I'm only doing what I think is best."

"Darling, you must stay on your journey and continue to write."

"I will, My Love."

As Oliver Reed's cabinet convened, the first order of discussion was the "Charm Offensive" and its impact.

"According to the media, Ms. Wolfe's speech went over big with the people," said Louis Summit, head of the Department of Optimism.

"Yes," said Agnes Triumpho, Secretary of Life, "I think her talk of advocating patience for our policies was exactly what was needed."

"However," said General Phillip Masters, Secretary of Defense, "how do you know we're getting the truth? How do you know if the polls are accurate and the media are reporting the facts?"

"The Fourth Estate is in the business of fact-finding and reporting results," said Sidney Voyeur, head of the Department of Knowledge. "They report the truth."

"Mr. Voyeur," said General Masters, "when did you start believing everything you've read and heard over the airwaves?"

After a brief discussion by the Cabinet members, it was decided to continue the Charm Offensive.

"It will pay great dividends," said President Reed.

"I feel it's a bankrupt policy, void of meaning, and the people see through it," said General Masters.

"The people are told what to believe and they follow," responded President Reed.

"Don't be so sure," said General Masters. "They aren't as ignorant as you think."

CHAPTER XXIX

The End of the Beginning

As I went from city to city and town to town, the people were organizing an attempt to go to the presidential mansion and physically remove President Oliver Reed from office. Following a successful coup d'etat, there would be a call for new elections, and only candidates who swore an allegiance to the Constitution and the inherent rights of the people would be eligible to run.

The leaders had arranged, subrosa, with General Phillip Masters, Secretary of Defense, for the military not to intervene in the planned coup.

The plans for the march were on a massive scale, with the possibility of millions of people flooding the nation's capital.

I called Cynthia Wolfe and gave her the date for her to meet me at a specific address in the capital, without mentioning the purpose of the day.

"Is it safe?" she asked.

"I can say only that it's a day that will long be remembered."

"Why do you say that?"

"You'll see." Then I hung up. As I did, I was a bit surprised she was seemingly unaware of the possible coup, but even if she seemed oblivious, I somehow knew she understood the importance of the day.

Cynthia met me the morning of the attempted coup and we hugged passionately.

By noon, we had walked to the presidential mansion and waited for a coup leader to enter the facility. He did and Cynthia and I, along with some others, followed. We marched up to Oliver Reed's ornate office. He wasn't there and Helene Wolfe, Cynthia's mother, sat in his chair.

Cynthia stared at her mother. She returned her stare.

"May I help you, ladies and gentleman?" Helene said.

"Where is President Reed?" the leader of the coup asked.

"He was aware of the possible coup d'etat and left this letter which I will now read: 'It is up to the intellectuals to remake the world. They will do so because it is only they who have the knowledge to lead. I'm resigning my office to unite with my fellow intellects to complete a refashioning of society for the benefit of our people and for mankind. Oliver Reed.'"

I replied, a bit startled, "The people must be free to decide and understand the meaning of freedom."

Meanwhile, Cynthia stared at her mother in disbelief. Then she said, "The folly of fools is perpetual."

"You've defined the problems of the ages," I replied.

"How about us?"

"You and I will live in our own paradise."

"Will it be a fool's paradise?"

"After what we've seen, it can't be. … We'll love one another and live our lives as we see fit."

"Then, My Darling, let's begin living," she said, as she embraced me, and I began to kiss her.

The Conformist and the Misfit

By Mark Carp

When opposites attract, the challenges can be unique.

Mark Carp

Dedication

To Aunt Celeste Cornblatt, who always had a comment

CHAPTER I

<u>The Bus Trip</u>

As I sat on the bus, looking out of the window, I thought about the talk I would be giving some four hours from now. Then I looked up and saw an attractive woman approach. She smiled easily and seemed to be brimming with self-confidence. She had brownish hair, was approximately 5'5" tall and exceptionally well built.

Even though the bus had fifty-four seats, and the odds of her sitting next to me were minimal, I hoped by some fortuitous chance her seat would be next to mine.

"Excuse me," she said, "is the seat next to you Number Twenty Two?"

"Yes," I said, smiling naturally.

I saw she was holding two pieces of luggage.

"May I help you place your belongings in the overhead compartment?" I asked.

"Thank you," she said, "but I can handle them."

I watched as she easily lifted the pieces and placed them in the compartment. Then, she sat down next to me, much to my delight.

"Are you going to New York," she asked, "to speak this afternoon at the Institute of Societal Advancement?"

I nodded assuredly, and asked, "How about you?"

"Yes," she said.

"What's your topic?" I asked.

"Journalism and the People."

"For or against?" I quipped.

"For," she smirked, seemingly unappreciative of my attempt at humor.

"What's your subject matter?"

"Economics as a Tool for the Betterment of Mankind."

"That's an interesting title," she said. "Say, are you an economist?"

"I claim to be," I quipped.

"How do you earn your living?" she asked.

"I'm a professor at a local college and do consulting on the side."

"Whom do you consult for?"

"Anyone who will hire me," I said, smiling.

"I take it you're an active journalist," I said.

"Yes."

"Whom do you write for?"

"I'm a columnist for the *Sentinel Times*."

"Say, that's a pretty wild group."

"What do you mean by that?" she snarled.

"I mean your editorial policy permeates the paper and how the news is reported."

"I disagree," she said. "We try to report the truth."

"Unfortunately, your version of truth differs substantially from mine."

"Before we get into a big argument," she said. "I would like to know your name."

"I'm Stephen Kaplan."

"And you are …?"

"Myra Foreman."

"Pleased to meet you," I said.

"I hope so," she replied. … "Anyway, I take it you're no fan of the *Sentinel*."

"Not in the least."

"Why?"

"Because every time an issue occurs, I know how the story will be slanted, what types of people will be quoted, and what your editorials will advocate."

"Maybe it's that way because we're right."

"And maybe it's that way because you're wrong, but you're too imbued with a philosophy that won't let you see the other side of an issue."

"Can you be more specific?"

"How about your continued push for a higher minimum wage?"

"Are you so cold-hearted that you would deny people basic human sustenance?"

"So what happens when the wage is raised to such a level you're eliminating a segment of the population, because of a lack of skill, from employment?"

"People need to be paid accordingly," Myra said.

"People need to be employed so they can earn a living wage, but they can't be employed if the cost of their employment exceeds their ability to produce."

"No wonder they call your profession the *Dismal Science*."

"Economics is not a science where the same remedies will necessarily produce the same outcomes."

"Then why is it called a science?"

"I suppose everyone is looking for respectability."

"Say ... you seem to have a sense of humor," Myra laughed.

"It beats being forever righteously angry. ... Perhaps your editors should learn how to smile a little, too."

Myra smirked and picked up a magazine.

"What happened to our conversation?" I asked.

"I didn't mean to be discourteous."

"Then please put down the magazine."

"Okay," she said.

"What do you like to do?"

"I have a full life: I play tennis, go to the theatre, swim, frequent the symphony and write a column."

"Ah, a highbrow."

"How about you, Steve?"

"Oh, I go to the track, play poker every night and I'm a regular at local casinos."

"Uh, I never would have imagined ..."

"I'm teasing you ... Actually, I like to do a lot of the same things you do."

"Is that a pickup line?"

"It isn't, but after we finish giving our *rousing* talks, perhaps we could have dinner together and then maybe, if you feel like it, we could go to a show. There are a lot of off-Broadway theatres I've attended and seen some terrific stuff."

"What kind of theatre interests you?"

"I enjoy drama. The kind that evokes real life and is earthy to the core."

"You seem to be an interesting guy."

"I'd like for you to come with me tonight to see if your instincts are correct."

Myra smiled but didn't answer.

CHAPTER II

Talk, Talk, Talk

We left the bus and I asked Myra if we could share a cab on the way to the Institute of Societal Advancement.

She smiled assuredly.

I soon hailed a cab and placed her luggage along with mine in the trunk.

"Thank you for being so helpful," she said.

"Not at all," I replied.

"I see we're both on a panel tomorrow to discuss 'The Individual and the State' and 'Social Responsibility and the Corporation.'"

"Yes," Myra replied.

"I hope you take it easy on me," I laughed.

"By the way, what is your view of the corporation having social responsibility?"

"Basically, the firm has one responsibility."

"What is that?"

"To earn a profit for its shareholders. It is they who own the company, and not some hypocritical politician or officious editor."

"Aren't you being a bit shortsighted?"

"Not in the least."

"But you're not being very virtuous."

"Actually, I am."

"How so?"

"If the corporation produces according to the needs of the people, it is they who receive the goods and services of the self-interested, profit-seeking firm, and these have become the sustenance of life. To me, that's virtue of the highest order, because one party is free to produce and the other has the freedom to purchase and consume."

"But corporations have exploited the people."

"If there was so much exploitation in the form of excess profits, competitors would seize the moment, enter the market, and lower prices, while still earning a profit, thus putting the exploiters out of business, or forcing them to charge less. ... You'd be better off if you understood the system and not look for collusion every five minutes."

"Somebody has to be the watchdog."

"To be a watchdog, you have to understand what you're watching."

"I think I do."

"I believe you don't."

At that moment, Myra turned her head and began to stare out of the window.

We soon arrived at the Institute, and the cab driver announced the fare.

As I reached into my pocket to pay it, Myra said, "Let me share it with you."

"I've got it," I replied. "Besides, I'll give the driver a nice tip so he won't feel exploited."

"Was that necessary?"

"I was just trying to be humorous."

"I'm not laughing."

"I've noticed."

I asked Myra if I could help carry her luggage into the building.

"I can handle it," she said.

"I thought if I could help you, you would give me a tip so I wouldn't feel exploited."

"Okay, okay I hear you."

"Frankly, my dear, I haven't said too much worth hearing."

"You've said plenty."

"I'd still like to take you to dinner tonight and say more."

"You may be succeeding in your quest. ... Uh, I do find you rather intriguing."

"What do you like to eat? ... but don't tell me you're a vegetarian."

"I'll take the Fifth Amendment on that one," Myra laughed.

"There's a nice Spanish restaurant in Chelsea."

"How are the vegetables?"

"I don't know, I avoid them at all costs."

"Stephen, if you don't eat your vegetables, you won't grow big and strong."

"Let me make a note of that," I smiled.

Once in the Institute, Myra and I were given a copy of today's program. She was to precede me as a speaker. Our speeches, based on our previous conversations, were rather predictable. She spoke of more corporate regulation in the name of equity and protecting the people. I took the opposite view: Let the people decide what they wish to purchase and have the firm supply these needs at a profit so it can stay in business.

Following the end of the program, where she and I were among four speakers, I asked her if we were on for dinner that evening.

She nodded and smiled.

I returned her beautiful smile.

CHAPTER III

<u>The Panel and Afterwards</u>

As we dined in the restaurant, I asked Myra, "Have you ever thought about the fact that two people can live in the same environment and have vastly different views on life?"

"I have."

"Why do you think that's so?"

"I look around and see exploitation and poverty, both of which need to be addressed."

"And I see how the needs of the people are being filled by firms which gauge demand and try to meet the wants of their customers in order to survive."

"Well, Stephen, what is your solution for the problems I suggest?"

"Let the people and the firms decide on the best course of action. In the end, that will produce the best result."

"But some people don't do well with freedom. They need to be counseled and provided for."

"So why be angry at corporations for conditions that are largely out of their control?"

Myra was silent and lifted her menu, giving me the impression she was hiding behind it, contemplating my words.

"Put the menu down," I said, "and let me see that pretty face of yours."

She did and smiled.

"You're very attractive," I said.

"Thank you," she replied.

"Anyway, you and I are on the same panel tomorrow to discuss the issues we've been discussing."

"But do you think things will ever improve?"

"They continue to improve."

"Why do you say that?"

"All you have to do is compare life today with what it was a hundred and two-hundred years ago. The difference is startling."

"But they need to improve more."

"So let the people and business remain free. That's the best prescription for societal advancement."

"But we need more planning to help the downtrodden."

"Has planning helped the downtrodden or has it kept them down?"

"Why do you say that?"

"Have the programs you seem to advocate lifted the people from poverty or have they become boondoggles that absorb resources without achieving the promised results?"

"To an extent what you've said is true."

"So why do more of the same in the expectation the results will be different?"

"But you can't sit idly by and see people get hurt."

"How do you know what you advocate is what the people need?"

After a moment of deafening silence, Myra said, "Perhaps we should change the subject."

"I'd love to."

"After dinner, maybe we can go to the theatre."

"Is there anything in particular that you would like to see?"

"Let me search my iPhone and see what's playing."

After I did, I said, "Here's something that may be worth viewing off Broadway."

"What is it?"

"It's a one-woman show based on the life of Zelda Fitzgerald, wife of F. Scott Fitzgerald."

"I wonder if it's depressing."

"Just because it may be depressing doesn't mean it's not worth seeing. ... Besides, I've seen some tremendous drama off Broadway. The producers can do a lot with a little."

"Interesting. I'll take you up on that."

"So it's a date," I laughed.

"Yes, an extension of the one we're on."

Following dinner I told Myra we could take the Subway to the theatre.

"Is it safe at night?" she asked.

"Should be. Besides it's fast and economical."

"Maybe we should take a cab."

"No, we'll take the Subway."

"But suppose we're accosted by hooligans."

"I'll protect you."

"But who is going to protect you?"

"I never thought of that … Maybe you can protect both of us."

"I don't think so," Myra said somberly.

Anyway, we took the Subway, got off a few blocks from the theatre, and walked to it.

"Here we are," I said, "safe and sound."

I purchased tickets for the both of us and we sat through the show.

As we left the theatre, I asked Myra what she thought of the play.

"I really enjoyed it," she said. "How about you?"

"I was absorbed by it from beginning to end."

Myra smiled at my comment and I said, "How about if we find a place for some dessert and coffee?"

"I'll do the coffee without the dessert. I'm watching my figure."

"I like watching it, too."

"Wasn't that a sexist comment?"

"Yes."

"Then why did you say it?"

"Because it's true."

"Oh," she said.

"Lighten up," I replied. "We're two people, enjoying each other's company. Don't look for problems."

Myra smiled, embarrassed, I assumed.

The following day, Myra and I sat on a panel which discussed income inequality, among other topics. When asked how I viewed this issue, I said, "Income inequality represents society's view of the worth of people. Some individuals are paid more because of the skills they seemingly possess. For instance, look how athletes, entertainers and corporate executives are compensated. This is as a result of supply and demand, where the most skillful are paid accordingly, and where employers and employees are free to agree to a level of income. It's quite simple when you come down to it."

When asked if teachers should be compensated more, I replied, "If there is an adequate supply of teachers at the current level of pay, an increase in wages would likely produce a surplus of educators followed by pressure to lower their income."

"Isn't that heartless?" I was asked.

I replied, "Who needs a surplus of teachers!"

Following the panel discussion, Myra asked, "How did it feel to be the misfit in the group?"

"I have my views," I replied. "I'm comfortable with what I've said."

"So you don't care if you draw the ire of attendees?"

"Not in the least."

"Well that's kind of noble of you."

"I'd rather be a misfit than conform for the sake of conformity. By the way, since the *Sentinel* prides itself on freedom of expression, how many journalists and columnists do you have who don't adhere to the philosophy of the paper?"

Myra smiled, embarrassed, but didn't answer.

Then, I replied, "The reason you can't answer is you have none, and if you ever had, I'm sure they're long gone. At most media, freedom of expression means if you don't conform, you're out. I don't find that particularly noble."

"Are you lecturing me?"

"Hardly, I'm only being truthful, and, quite often, truthfulness of expression is lacking in most media."

"Does that include the outlets you read and listen to?"

Then I stammered, "P-r-o-b-a-b-l-y."

CHAPTER IV

I've Met Someone

Following the panel discussion, she and I walked back to the hotel.

"I'll meet you in the lobby in a half hour and we'll walk a couple of blocks to catch the bus," I said.

Myra nodded.

"I hope we can sit together," she said.

"I've arranged that."

"How?"

"I've called the bus company and asked that our seats be side by side."

Myra smiled widely and I returned her winsome smile.

We met in the lobby and I asked her if I could carry one of her bags.

"Thank you," she replied, "but it won't be necessary."

We came to the bus and boarded it. As the bus pulled away, I asked her, "How is it that an attractive woman like you isn't married?"

"I'm separated," she said.

"I'm sorry to hear that."

"He wasn't right for me. It was all wrong from the beginning."

"So I assume there's no chance for reconciliation."

"Not a chance," she said bluntly.

"How about you?" Myra followed.

"I've been in some relationships, but they didn't work out. ... It's tough to find Miss Right."

"You're an attractive, bright guy. There will be plenty of opportunities for you, and you'll find the right one."

"Anyway, I've enjoyed your company. If you're not busy next weekend, I could get tickets to the symphony and we could have dinner first."

"What pieces will be performed?"

"Tchaikovsky's 'Romeo and Juliet Overture' and the 'Pathetique,' his sixth symphony."

"How about if I let you know."

"How about if I need to know in the next thirty seconds."

"What's the rush?"

"Because I'd like to be with you next weekend."

"Is my thirty seconds up?"

"Yes," I said, checking my watch.

"May I have another minute to think about this?"

"If you wish, but I'm timing that, too."

Myra smiled and said, "Okay, it's a date."

Then I returned her smile.

Myra and I talked nonstop on our way back home. Though our views on politics and economics were far apart, we conversed easily.

Then we began to discuss a number of other subjects, including literature and art. On those areas of discussions, some of our views were aligned, others not. Still, whether we agreed, each respected the other's opinion.

As we got off the bus and I walked her to her car, I said, "I'll call you this week to firm things up for the weekend." She smiled when I said that.

We came to her car and she opened her trunk. I placed her bags inside of it and she closed the trunk door.

"How do you want to end the evening?" I asked.

She put her arms around me and hugged me in a way that was passionate and strong. I reciprocated, doing the same.

"I could get to like you," she quipped.

"I already do," I said seriously.

Two days later, I picked up a copy of the *Sentinel* and read her column. The headline was: "The Attraction of Diversity."

Then I began to read what she had written: "This past weekend, I met a man on a bus ride to the Institute of Societal Advancement in New York City, where we were both speakers and panelists on weighty subject matter. As an economist, his approach to the ills of society was almost completely different from mine. No wonder it is called the *Dismal Science*. Nonetheless, he took me to dinner that evening and we ate at a delightful Spanish restaurant, and, following that, we saw a spellbinding play about Zelda Fitzgerald, the wife of author F. Scott Fitzgerald.

"I found my date totally engaging and a joy to be with. He has already asked me out for a second date, which I've gladly accepted.

"We seem to represent the best of what diversity is supposed to be. We're together because we want to be, not because we're part of a social experiment whose formula is have enough forced diversity even if the people despise one another and social friction results.

"Also, I found him rather attractive with his jet-black hair, swarthy complexion, athletic frame and six-foot height."

I called Myra after I read her column and complimented her on it.

She replied, "I'm looking forward to the weekend."

"I am too," I replied. "Besides, I didn't know I was so sexy."

"No comment," she laughed.

CHAPTER V

Hooligans and Me

Myra and I had been dating for a couple of weeks, when I was scheduled to speak at a local college on "Positive Economics and the Rise of Mankind."

When my appearance at the school was publicized, protest groups began to organize to deny my appearance.

Myra went to the school to interview Joel Raskin, a leader of one of the groups. She sat with him and asked, "Why do you object to Dr. Kaplan speaking at the school which you attend?"

"Because his views are harmful."

"How so?"

"They keep some people down and promote inequality."

"Because of that, he shouldn't be allowed to speak?"

"Why should we give a voice to people who are hurtful?"

"Why don't you listen with your own ears to see if some of what he says makes sense?"

"Everyone knows his views are out of touch and malignant."

"Like who?"

"The professors at this university."

"Could they be wrong and Professor Kaplan be right?"

"I don't think so."

"What is to be gained if he ascends to the podium and is shouted down?"

"Our statement is heard!"

"What precisely is your statement?"

"Absurdism isn't allowed."

"Who is being absurd?" Myra asked.

As it was, as I began to speak, I was pelted with debris and jeered every time I made a statement. After a futile attempt at speaking, I left the stage, disgusted and angry, with epithets such as "fascist," "bastard" and "bigot" ringing in my ears. As I walked out of the building, I ran into Myra, who was covering my speech for the *Sentinel*.

"I guess your paper is happy that its readers have seemingly had the last word at my attempt at speaking," I said.

"Don't be absurd," Myra snapped.

"I'm sorry, I'm just a bit angry and upset. I shouldn't have said what I have just said."

"You have every right to be angry. Nobody likes to be in such a bizarre trap."

"Let's get out of here," I said, "and let these fools and 'educators' bask in their own folly."

Myra nodded assuredly.

"Let's take my car and we'll go to a coffee shop off campus," I replied.

Myra concurred and we drove to an eatery some four blocks from the school. Inside the shop I saw a poster announcing my talk.

As Myra and I looked at it, she said, "I know the food here is better than how you were received."

"It better be," I snapped loudly.

"Calm down," Myra said, grasping my hand.

"Please let go," I ranted. She did. Then I got up, disgusted, and began to pace in the restaurant. As I did, Myra asked, "Do you wish to stay here?"

"I'll be okay. I just need a few minutes to cool off."

"Take your time," Myra said.

Soon, I regained my composure and sat with her.

"You know," I said, "I tried to speak on an intellectual basis about what works best, and I'm shouted down by a bunch of hooligans who believe they're being intellectually correct. What am I missing?"

"You're not missing anything, Steve."

"Then who encourages these fools besides the professors and the media?"

"My paper doesn't encourage such things."

"Oh, I believe it does."

"How?"

"People like me are never given the proper audience. All you do is run to people, for quotes and analysis, who are critical of positions that I and others of my ilk take. Then you repeatedly print their comments as if these are words from on high. Frankly, most of the critics don't know what the hell they're talking about."

"We're not as bad as you say," Myra replied.

"You're not? Why don't you start reading your own paper!"

"But, of course, I do."

"Then you're not an objective reader. There is another world you're completely missing. You're too close to the source to see the problem."

At that moment, Myra was silent and a waitress came to take our order.

We ate in silence, both upset over how the evening had gone. Following our meal, I told Myra, "I'll take you back to your car."

"Are you okay?" she asked.

"I'm okay, just a bit agitated."

As we drove to her car, she asked, "Would you want to stay with me this evening?"

I smiled widely when she said that.

"That's the first time you smiled this evening," she said.

"That's the first thing I've had to smile about," I replied.

CHAPTER VI

Responding, Relating and Planning the Immediate Future

Myra and I woke up and I said, "That was some ending to an unanticipated evening."

"Yes, you do know how to *end* things."

"I do like to give."

"And, I did like to receive what you were giving."

"I suppose you're not going to write about our previous night's escapades in your next column."

"I might intimate something is going on between us."

"Say, am I part of the serial?"

"I wouldn't put it exactly that way, but so far so good."

"So our story keeps evolving."

"Yes, positively."

"So I'm not so dismal, even though I'm a member of the Dismal Science."

"You are perhaps the least-dismal person I know."

"Come here," I said.

At that moment, I grabbed Myra and we commenced another round of lovemaking.

We reveled in each other's arms and our passion was uncontrolled. When we reached our climax, both of us shrieked in delight. Then we stared in each other's eyes, each smiling widely.

"What's your column going to be on today?" I asked.

"I'm not sure," Myra replied.

"How about: 'It's Good for a Man and a Woman to Return to the Cave.'"

I can think it, I just can't write it."

"Why? Is it because you and your readers all hide behind a façade, pretending to be something you're not?"

"Must you always be so blunt?"

"I don't mean to be. It's just my nature."

"Well, it's not so terrible. Besides, you do have a rough sense of integrity, and I like that."

"On a different matter, thanks for trying to assuage my feelings from my attempt at speaking last night. I was quite upset."

"Nobody should be treated like that. You didn't deserve those kinds of indignities."

"Oh well," I laughed, "I like our way of returning to the cave more so than my critics' way."

"At least our way is more fun," Myra said, joining me in my laughter.

"I'm going to get dressed," Myra followed. "I've got to get to the office and do a column."

"I've got a graduate seminar to teach at 10 A.M."

"On what?"

"On why Trade Imbalances are often much to do about nothing."

"Sounds kind of dry to me," Myra said.

"Oh, well," I replied, "I'll keep my powder dry – just for you."

"I think I'd like that."

I smiled and began to dress.

When Myra returned to her office, she sat at her word processor and began to type: "Last night I witnessed a horrific example of hooliganism at Carleton University, which prides itself on freedom of expression and being an incubator of ideas.

"When Stephen Kaplan, Ph.D., tried to speak on his subject of the evening, 'Positive Economics and the Rise of Mankind,' he was jeered with expletives and pelted with debris. He was unable to deliver his remarks and left the podium disgusted and distraught.

"Perhaps it's time for the University to examine its mission and decide if it's fulfilling it.

"If last night was any kind of example, the answer clearly it is not."

When Myra finished her column, she called and read the opening to me.

"What's there to say," I said, "except it was nothing more than a disgusting exhibition and the purveyors must be held responsible."

"I'm sure they will be."

"I doubt it," I replied, "perhaps at the University they will be feted as heroes."

"I think you're being overly cynical."

"I doubt I'm being cynical enough."

"Anyway, would you care to join me for lunch?"

"I'd love to," I said.

As Myra left for lunch, two reporters began to talk. Joel Franklin said to Peter Engels, "Look how good Myra looks. She seems to have a glow about her."

"Maybe she's getting very serious with someone."

"Probably, she's scowling less and smiling more."

"As she does that," Engels said, "she's even more attractive than usual."

"I agree," Franklin replied.

As Myra and I sat for lunch, she asked, "How did your seminar go?"

"Rather well," I replied. "I lectured. Then we had some high-level discussions on the pros and cons of what I had said. I've got a group of good students who are attentive and absorbed."

"I'd like to think my readers are also absorbed and attentive."

"That's the hope, but are they critical thinkers or blind followers?"

"I hope they are critical thinkers. After all, I'm a person with an opinion, and there are other opinions besides mine."

"I'm glad you feel as you do. None of us knows everything."

"That's for sure."

"Although sometimes when I'm around journalists I think they feel wisdom begins and ends with them."

"I suppose you could say that about people in all professions," Myra replied.

"On a lighter note, what would you like to do this weekend?"

"You suggest something."

"How about a nice dinner and then we could to dancing?"

"I'd love to," Myra replied.

CHAPTER VII

A Marriage Proposal

Following dinner, Myra and I went to the Starlight Room, located on the top floor of a twenty-two story building, where a combo was playing and food and drinks were being served.

As we sat, the combo introduced a Gershwin piece, "Someone to Watch Over Me."

"Shall we?" I asked.

Myra nodded assuredly.

As we came to the dance floor, the vocalist sang: "There's a somebody I'm longing to see, I hope that he turns out to be someone who'll watch over me."

When I heard those lyrics I smiled widely at my date. She returned my smile and then she held me tightly. I was in ecstasy, not wanting the song to end. As Myra continued to hold me tightly, I knew she felt the same.

When the music ended, we stood together on the dance floor, maintaining our embrace.

"Uh, I think it's time to sit down," I said.

Myra was silent, and I escorted her from the dance floor.

As we sat, she said, "Such beautiful lyrics, such a beautiful moment. I wanted us to be frozen in time."

"A beautiful wish from a beautiful lady," I replied.

"Will such lyrics and music ever be duplicated?"

"They can't be," I replied, "but as long as we're together, we can have moments like this."

"I love being with you, Steve."

"I feel the same."

At that moment, a waitress came to our table and asked us if we wanted to order. Myra said she wanted a glass of red wine. "I'll have the same," I replied.

After the waitress left, I said, "I would like to be with you eternally. I would like to marry you."

Myra was silent, apparently unable to reply.

"Well, what are you thinking?" I asked.

"I don't know, Steve. Marriage is such a big step."

"I think we would be fabulous together."

"But we're so different."

"Maybe it's true: Opposites attract."

"But what if they don't?"

"We will, I know it," I replied.

"You know I'm scared."

"Why?"

"Because my first marriage was such a fiasco."

"We're all apprehensive. It comes from experience and living life. But I think our life together would be beautiful."

"I don't know if I'm ready, now."

"What happened to the columnist who writes with such certitude?"

"I suppose it's easy to be brave with your opinions. It's quite another to put them into practice."

"That doesn't mean you shouldn't try. Life is about probing and making the necessary modifications along the way. I know we would find happiness and be together forever."

"I'm going to need time to think about this. ... Marriage is a huge, huge step."

"No matter what your decision is, I love you."

"I love you too, Steve. You're a wonderful person."

"I don't want us to part."

My date smiled but didn't answer.

CHAPTER VIII

I've Become a "Hostile" Witness

Myra and I kept dating and, intermittently, I would bring up marriage. Although she seemed more willing to consider the idea, Myra could not accept my thought of a nuptial.

During one of our dates, she brought up the fact I would be testifying before the House of Delegates Committee on Economic Matters on behalf of the Chamber of Commerce against a proposed state law that called for a rise in the Minimum Wage.

"I guess you're aware," Myra said, "that forces will be arrayed against you and paint you as some kind of Neanderthal."

"I've had plenty of practice with such nonsense, including the *Sentinel*."

"Okay, okay. I wish you wouldn't bring up the paper I write for."

"I guess it's a conditional response, because I know what will happen next."

"I know you know, so why do you repeat the obvious?"

"I can't help it."

"Well, try to," Myra said angrily.

"I'll try if my critics try."

"You know that won't happen. They're literally trained to respond in certain ways."

"Here again, you're speaking of your editorial writers."

"Uh, I would appreciate it if we didn't go through this again."

"Then why did you bring it up?"

"Because I care so deeply for you and don't wish to see you get hurt."

"Well, if you care so much, why can't you accept my proposal of marriage?"

"I'm just afraid. I'm so scarred from my previous one."

"Eventually, scars must heal."

Myra didn't answer.

* * *

Myra covered my testimony on raising the minimum wage before the Committee on Economic Matters.

As I entered the capitol building, signs carried by picketers read: "Be Humane, Raise The Minimum Wage" and "Professor Kaplan Is But Another Mouthpiece For Keeping People Down."

After I took the witness stand and was sworn in, Delegate Rodger Cummings asked, "What is your position on raising the minimum wage?"

"It shouldn't be raised."

"Why?"

"Because if it is raised, you may create unemployment among jobholders and deny employment to those who seek work."

"Why is this so?"

"Because people could lack the skills to be employed at the rate of pay that the Legislature may fix."

"Then, Professor Kaplan, what is your remedy?"

"Eliminate the minimum wage altogether."

"Why is this preferable?"

"Because you would achieve greater employment."

"Why do you say that?"

"Because classical economics has taught us supply and demand meet at a price. There is a demand curve for labor much in the way there is a demand curve for other commodities."

"So you would be content to see people employed at slave wages?"

"No, I would like to see people employed at a wage the market can bear. Further, I would like for the employees to develop skills, either by education or experience, so the market can afford them a higher wage."

"I have no more questions, Professor Kaplan."

I was next questioned by Delegate Althea Brown.

"Professor Kaplan, what is your view on international trade?"

"I'm completely for it."

"Why?"

"Because it gives consumers more choice and it creates more competition among suppliers of goods and services."

"Suppose international trade creates unemployment in local industries?"

"Delegate Brown, maybe you should be asking, 'Isn't it preferable that because of international trade more and better goods and services are being offered at cheaper prices?' After all, we're, at some point, consumers."

"But what should I tell my constituents who have become unemployed because of foreign competition?"

"Tell them what I've just told you."

"Delegate Gerald Manchon, the chairman of the Committee on Economic Matters, said, "It's time for a recess. These hearings will reconvene at 1 P.M."

I approached Delegate Manchon and said, "I was advised that I would be excused from testifying by noon. I have a graduate seminar to teach at 2:30 P.M. and I must get back to campus."

"I'm afraid that will be impossible, Dr. Kaplan."

"I'm sorry I'm going to leave in accordance with my previous understanding."

"Then you may go, but the Committee may issue a subpoena for you to return."

"If a subpoena comes, I'll decide if it's appropriate."

"If you ignore the subpoena, you'll be held in contempt."

"Delegate Manchon, are you turning this into a vendetta?"

The delegate refused to reply and I left, distraught.

CHAPTER IX

Myra, the State and Me

I was soon subpoenaed, to reappear before the Economic Matters Committee. As I was having dinner with Myra, we discussed the subpoena.

"You know," I said, "I'm fodder for the fools who wish to play up my appearance. The possibility of my showing up has become a bigger story than what I have to say."

"Are you going to appear?"

"I'm not sure."

"If you don't, you'll be playing into their hands."

"And if I do, I'll be a participant in a feeding frenzy."

"I suppose," Myra said forlornly, "you're damned if you do and damned if you don't."

"Well the mob is getting what it wants and the *Sentinel* is among its ringleaders."

"Okay, okay let's not go through this again."

"Why? This is a paper that gives credence to the worst among us in the name of perpetuating diverse opinions; yet, it is content to use a drumbeat of smear tactics against me and people of my ilk."

"I must say you're not entirely wrong."

"Then if you had principles, you would resign from the *Sentinel*."

"I'm trying to correct things from the inside."

"You're not doing a very good job. ... Besides, why don't you tell me the truth?"

"Which is?"

"You make a good living as a columnist and you're unwilling to give up the status and notoriety your column has brought you."

"I'm not denying what you have just said."

"At least there is someone on the paper who is honest."

"Okay, okay ..."

To avoid a hassle, I decided to again appear before the Economic Matters Committee. However, prior to any testimony I would give, I would be allowed to read my opening statement.

I was sworn in and began to read: "Ladies and Gentlemen, I've been subpoenaed to appear before this body, not for what I have to say because you know my positions. Rather, I'm part of a staged exhibition designed to portray me as an evildoer and you as self-righteous protectors of the people's interest. As a result, you're nothing more than duplicitous ringleaders of a mob you have helped to perpetuate. At some point, your constituents would be far better served if you would educate them and not try to be their Messiah."

I then looked up at Delegate Gerald Manchon, chairman of the Economic Matters Committee.

He said, "Are you finished with your opening statement?"

I nodded assuredly.

"Then we will proceed with the questioning," Delegate Manchon followed.

However, none of the delegates on the committee said anything.

As the silence became deafening, I said, "Since, apparently, no one has anything to ask me, I would like to be excused, as I have important matters to attend to."

Delegate Manchon looked at his committee members who were rigidly silent. Then he said softly, "You may go."

I nodded and left.

Myra, who was covering my testimony as a columnist for the *Sentinel*, met me in the lobby.

"I never heard anyone under oath speak to the Legislature like that," she said.

"They deserve it and the delegates need to act responsibly. They are representatives of the people, not their ringleaders."

"I'm going back to the office to do my column."

"I'll talk to you later," I said, and I kissed her on the cheek.

When Myra returned to the office, she began to compose her column: "In the world we live in, there are propagandists and people of principle. Stephen Kaplan, who holds a doctorate in economics, is among the principled. He is unafraid to state his position and doesn't need to read poll results to decide how he's to think. Moreover, he will clearly explain his rationale for any position he holds to anyone who wishes to converse with him, including the State Legislature.

"In a nutshell, he's against state interference in the economy through such measures as wage and price controls, including setting a minimum wage; tariffs, and excessive regulations, and favors Individualism and Freedom."

Myra called me to read the opening lines of her column. I thanked her and asked, "When will I see you again?"

"Whenever you wish," she said.

CHAPTER X

Father, Daughter and Me

Myra invited me to have dinner with her and her father, Samuel Foreman, a retired college professor of philosophy, at his condominium.

She and I entered his unit and Myra's father hugged her lovingly and said, "How's my famous daughter?"

"Still grinding out columns," she laughed.

"Come, come, my child, you do more than grind out copy. Your work is quite perceptive."

"Thank you, Daddy."

"Daddy, I want you to meet Stephen Kaplan, the fellow whom I've told you about and who I've been seeing regularly."

"Dr. Kaplan needs no introduction. He seems to have become unintentionally famous."

"I can assure you," I said, "I seek neither fame nor notoriety, only acceptance by my peers based on my work."

"That's the proper attitude, young man," Samuel replied. "In life, people's perception of who you are and who you really are can be as different as night and day."

"How well I know, Dr. Foreman."

"Please cut the formalities, Steve, and call me Sam."

"Okay."

"Why don't we sit in the den until dinner is ready?"

"Certainly, Daddy."

"Fine with me," I replied.

As we sat, Sam asked me about my views and I replied, "My views stem from the individualism and freedom of the people to plot the best course. I'm a great believer in Adam Smith's 'Invisible Hand' as the best means for society to grow and prosper."

"What happens if the Invisible Hand fails?"

"Over time, it is a philosophy that has produced the best results. It's the course of action that allows mankind to reach the summit of his existence."

"Interesting," Samuel said.

"Let's keep the evening light," Myra replied. "I want to enjoy my company."

"Steve and I will enjoy ourselves by discussing situations and issues that are pertinent to our views and beliefs. Isn't that so, Steve?"

"Whatever you say," I laughed, "I wish to keep my host happy."

"Okay, okay," Myra said.

"Tell me, Steve, what is your view of academia in America?" Sam asked.

"Do you want me to be blunt?"

"Yes."

"Here we go," Myra said, exasperated.

"I wonder if sometimes we're more interested in indoctrination than education," I replied.

"So what's your solution?" Sam said.

"It's incumbent on all students to go out in the real world and learn about life."

"In spite of their education?"

"Yes. There's an old saying: If you want to learn, don't go to school."

"Does that apply to you?"

"It applies to all enlightened people."

"So you're enlightened?"

"I'd like to think so."

"And how did you become enlightened?"

"I experienced the real world."

"After you experienced it, what were your views on your extensive education?"

"Some I accepted and some I rejected."

"Whom did you accept?"

"Milton Friedman, Irving Fisher, Frederich Hayek, Adam Smith, Joseph Shumpeter, David Hume, Alfred Marshall, David Ricardo, and Jean Baptiste Say, among others."

"And whom did you reject?"

"Thomas Malthus, Karl Marx and John Maynard Keynes, among the many."

"Why Keynes? Didn't he help cure the Great Depression?"

"Some of his economic philosophy is pure nonsense, and no he didn't help cure the Great Depression. Moreover, he didn't understand the cause of the Great Depression."

"Which was?" Sam asked.

"A lack of liquidity in the financial system caused by bank runs and a failure of confidence. After all, money is created and destroyed in the banking system and the Federal Reserve didn't take the proper steps to create the needed liquidity in the system."

"And it was as simple as that?"

"In my view, yes."

"How about government programs such as the Civilian Conservation Corps and the Agricultural Adjustment Administration?"

"Not in the least. As for government employment through such programs as the CCC, there is a saying: 'You can't create prosperity by digging holes and filling them in.' Anyone can understand this."

"Except academics?"

"You've said it."

"So, in your view, *Dogma* has triumphed over facts."

"To a large extent, what you've said is true."

"And what is your solution?"

"I think the way I want. Let others think the way they wish."

"How about public works as something that could reverse a lagging trend in the business cycle?"

"I think there are a lot of myths associated with that philosophy."

"How so?"

"Do you know how long it takes to build a major highway or erect a bridge?"

"Obviously, many, many years."

"So how do you know where we'll be in the business cycle by the time legislation to perform such construction is passed? In other words from proposing, legislation, planning, construction and completion, you could be through two or more business cycles. Moreover, there is always the danger of building something that is not really needed and spending too much on it because of trying to court the vote of organized labor."

"What is your solution for public works?"

"Build things as needed, not for the sake of trying to manage the business cycle."

"So you believe in *laissez-faire* and letting the market take its course?"

"I think that is a better solution than trying to manage the unmanageable."

"Daddy," Myra interrupted, "when will you and Stephen finish your conversation? I'm feeling left out."

"We're finished, my dear," Sam said.

"Excuse me," Dr. Foreman, "I'm ready to serve dinner," Dinah Jefferson, the housekeeper, said.

"Shall we adjourn to the dinner table?" Sam asked.

"I'm all for that," I said.

"When we get there, let's keep the conversation light," Myra offered.

"Okay," Sam replied. "I won't disappoint my favorite person."

The conversation at the dinner table was fairly light, centering on Myra's and Sam's friends and relatives. Following dessert and coffee, we again retired to Sam's den, conspicuous for its hundreds of shelved books, some of which he had authored.

Sam said, "If the media and politicians continue to be rough on you, I know you have an advocate in my daughter."

"Once the avalanche of public opinion and misinformation starts, everyone can be swept up in it, including my defenders. There will be little room for critical thinking. There will only be room for unthinking, repetitive criticism, and my defenders will suffer scorn and possible ostracism."

"So you don't have confidence in a free press ferreting out the truth."

"The way news is reported generally follows the outlet's editorial opinion. In my view, you either fall in line or go."

CHAPTER XI

An Imitation of Life?

As Myra and I drove away from her father's residence, she said, "You continue to make it abundantly clear that you have little respect for my profession."

"Why should I? It is made up of a lot of people who tow the line to move up the totem pole."

"You're being far too simplistic."

"We'll see," I replied. "Those who may try to defend me may take the arrow meant for me."

"Why must you be so harsh?"

"Because someone has to. Besides, most people, including journalists, side with issues because of perceptions, not facts."

"So you're saying it's hard for a journalist to leave the reservation."

"Not unless they want to be 'scalped.'"

"We'll see," Myra replied matter-of-factly.

"Anyway, I enjoyed your father's company. He seems to be thoughtful and let me air my views."

"Yes, he's always been that way. He's a grown-up."

"There seems to be a shortage of them these days."

"Enough of such talk, Steve. ... What do you want to do now?"

"We can go to the Nostalgia Theatre."

"What's playing there?"

The Fountainhead.

"Ah, the story of Howard Roark, who, because of his convictions, would stand against everyone, if necessary."

"And don't forget Dominique Francon, who wanted to love him, but feared an intimate relationship because she knew what the world would do to him. ... Does that sound like us?"

"I suppose," Myra replied, "life can imitate art."

"Yes," I said, "it can and often does, but, one day, I feel, things will work out between us."

Myra didn't answer, and I didn't comment on her silence.

We were soon at the theatre and I purchased the tickets. Then we watched the film with rapt attention.

Following the movie, we stopped at an eatery called Serendipity for dessert and coffee.

"What did you think of the movie?" I asked.

"Intriguing on a number of levels," Myra replied.

"In some respects, I thought I was watching our relationship play out before us."

"Life, as the movie indicated, is filled with a myriad of choices."

"No doubt, but to feel good about one's self, you have to be true to your convictions."

"The dilemma," Myra replied, "is that truth can kill."

"So can cowardice."

After a pause, Myra said, "Perhaps we should change the subject."

"Okay. What do you want to do next weekend?" I asked.

"I wouldn't mind returning to this theatre. Please check your iPhone to see what's playing next."

"It's *Duck Soup* with the Marx Brothers."

"What's that about?"

"Insanity in government."

"Interesting," Myra replied.

"Yes," I said, "with our experience we should feel right at home."

Myra smiled wistfully, but didn't reply.

"Where to now?" I asked.

"Let's go back to my place."

"I'm all for that," I said.

"Perhaps," I thought to myself, "was Myra my Dominique Francon? If so, I wanted our story to end happily. ... I wanted life to imitate art."

CHAPTER XII

<u>A Day at the Beach</u>

I continued to see Myra non-stop, and I enjoyed our dates: The things we did, our conversations, and, in particular, the uncontrolled passion of our lovemaking.

I, at times, brought up marriage, which she continually rebuffed.

One day I asked her about her first marriage and she began to spill her guts out. Myra said, "It was all wrong from the beginning. I did what I thought I was supposed to do, not what I *should* have done."

"How so?" I asked.

"Like my father, he was a college professor in the humanities."

"Were you trying to marry your father?"

"I just thought …?

"Thought what?" I asked, breaking the silence.

"Well, I wrote for a living, and he wrote and taught for a living. I believed we were a suitable match. It would be a union of two thoughtful people."

"So what happened?"

"Everything possible."

"If you wish, please elaborate."

"Okay ... He cared only about his opinions and thought his wisdom was infinite. He abused me emotionally. Then there was his affair with a graduate student. I tried to repair our marriage and we sought counseling. We went a couple of times and he said he would change his ways."

"Then what happened?"

"Guess."

"Nothing changed."

"But you haven't heard the other sordid details."

"Please explain."

"Okay. He got the graduate student pregnant, and he paid for her abortion. Eventually, the administration found out and he was relieved of his faculty position. By then, I had had enough. We quickly agreed to a divorce and settlement and I moved on. So here I am."

"And you're still scarred from your experience?"

"Yes, wouldn't you be?"

"I guess so. But I'm not he, and I'm not a beast."

"I know you're not and I do care for you so deeply."

"And I care for you equally as deeply and one day I know things will work out between us."

Following that exchange, Myra quickly changed the subject, saying she had a busy day tomorrow and had to return to her apartment. I drove her there in silence, and we had a superficial good-night kiss. Though disappointed how the evening had ended,

I understood her feelings. I called her the next day in the office and asked how she felt.

"Much better," she said. "I'm glad I told you my tale of woe."

"Confession is good for the soul."

"It can be," she replied.

"I'm here for you," I said, "and I know you're here for me."

"Thank you, Steve. ... Uh, let me get back to work."

"I'll call you tomorrow and we'll make plans for the weekend."

"I always look forward to being with you."

"You know I love you."

"You know I love you too, Steve."

When I called her, I suggested during the upcoming weekend we could take a trip and go kayaking.

"I've never done that," Myra protested, "is it difficult?"

"No, it takes five or ten minutes to get the hang of it. It's pretty simple," I replied. "Besides, there is a nice hotel where we would stay and a lot of good restaurants, serving traditional food, nearby."

"I thought you were supposed to go to shul this Saturday."

"Well, they will do the prayers, Torah and Haftarah without me."

"Don't forget the sermon."

"That too," I laughed. "Besides, when you see this part of the state with its creeks, beach and bay, you'll feel spiritual."

"That may be good for a change, away from the angst of urban living and implausible issues."

"Besides," I said, "it may make for an interesting column, and, as they say, variety is the spice of life. Also, your readers would perhaps appreciate another side of you."

"Yeah," she said sarcastically, "I'll be known as the Nature Girl of the Newsroom."

"Well, your paper is a big proponent of environmentalism. Now you can speak from firsthand knowledge about preserving Mother Nature."

"Must you always make with the digs!"

"I can't help it. Sometimes I think the *Sentinel* is staffed by people who support issues they know nothing about. It's the triumph of clichés unmoored from reason."

"Are you finished?"

"It sounds like I should be," I laughed.

"Yes, you should be," Myra said emphatically.

Anyway, I picked her up that Saturday morning and we left for the beach.

We drove for an hour and fifteen minutes and reached the hotel. I carried our luggage to the room after we had checked in. We were both hungry and had breakfast in the hotel dining room. Following that, we returned to our room and called to rent a kayak. We then changed into our bathing suits and put T-shirts on. "I like looking at you better without your T-shirt," I said.

"If you're good, there may be ample opportunity for that later."

"Suppose I'm bad?"

"Oh, I don't discriminate."

"I like when you have a sense of humor," I said.

We walked to the kayak rental area and Mike, an employee, asked if we had done this before. I told him I had but my date hadn't. However, I said, "I'll be responsible for her."

He accepted my explanation, gave us life jackets, and we got into the boat. He shoved us off and I told Myra, "Watch how I row and imitate my stroke." She nodded and in a short time we were rowing in unison. We were soon in a creek where we saw ducks, beautiful vegetation and graceful trees.

"Isn't this something," I said. "It's the perfection of Mother Nature."

"I've never seen you so serene," Myra replied.

"If you can't be serene here, you can't be it anywhere. ... How about you, are you enjoying yourself?"

"More that I would have imagined," she replied.

We rowed for an hour, then brought the boat back.

"How was your trip?" Mike asked.

"Sensational," I said.

"Wonderful," Myra replied.

As we walked back to the hotel, I asked her if she wanted to go kayaking tomorrow.

"Yes," she said emphatically.

"When we get back, we'll have lunch," I said.

"Okay. What's good?"

"Shrimp, crab cakes, burgers, salads, it's all delicious."

We returned to the hotel, went to the restaurant, sat outside under an umbrella and ordered. I had a crab cake and she ate steamed shrimp. I had some of hers and she ate some of mine.

Following lunch, we drove to the beach in the bay area, rented an umbrella and chairs, went into the water, and began to swim.

"You're a real Esther Williams," I said, "and just as pretty."

Myra blushed from my words and then smiled beautifully.

"How about if we race?" I said.

"You're on," she replied, answering the challenge. "Where to?" she asked.

"The pier," I said.

"Who will give the start?"

"You can."

"Ready, set, go," she exclaimed.

We swam to the pier and arrived simultaneously.

"I guess we can call it a tie," she said, disappointed. "Would you want to try again?"

"Maybe later," I said.

"Chicken," she laughed.

When she said that, I playfully dunked her head under water.

She rose laughing and said, "Is your motto: If you can't beat 'em, drown 'em!"

"I'll let you know after our next race."

"You always were thoughtful."

"I try," I said.

We left the water, returned to our umbrella and sat, holding hands.

"I'm having a wonderful time," Myra said.

"It's so pretty here, I feel spiritual," I replied.

"More so than in shul?"

"It's a different feeling but both have their place. How about you?"

"I'm happy here and with you."

Following our stay at the beach, we had a nice seafood dinner at a restaurant overlooking the bay. We returned to the hotel, exhausted, got into bed and fell asleep in each other's arms.

The following day we repeated our activities of the previous day: Good meals, kayaking and swimming. That evening, as we drove home, I asked Myra, "What do you think?"

"When will we come back?" she smiled.

"Soon," I hoped. "But tomorrow it's back to the grind."

"How well I know," she said.

CHAPTER XIII

Publishing and Perishing?

As I sat in my office, I got a call from my publisher, Xanadu Press. I was told my newest book, *The Individual and the Economy*, was ready for its release. We made plans for the release party, which would occur on the last weekend of the month.

I called Myra and told her about the upcoming event.

She said, "You didn't tell me you were writing another book."

"Well, I don't like talking about such things."

"Why?"

"These are very personal matters and I put so much into it, I have trouble speaking of it."

"Anyway, what's it about?"

"In the main, it's about society being better off when the populace pursues personal gain, away from the restraints of rules, regulations and doctrinaire, suffocating planning."

"Do you cite examples?"

"Of course."

"Can you give me some?"

"Look around and see where many of the things we take for granted come from."

"Such as?"

"Computers, airplanes, telephones, electric lights, television, etc. Frankly, there are too many to mention, and these inventions weren't the product of a government-mandated five-year plan, but were the result of an individual or individuals pursuing their self-interest."

"Your book sounds interesting."

"It's my highly personal statement, my magnum opus, backed by numerous examples."

"You know your critics will lash out against your work."

"Does that include the *Sentinel*?"

"I hope not, but I can't be sure."

"Well one thing I'm sure of is that the mob knows no bounds."

"Please, enough of such talk, let's celebrate your achievement."

"If it were only so simple."

Myra and I said our good-byes and she went back to writing her column. When she finished it, Myra called and read me the opening: "This past weekend, my significant other and I took a trip to an area of our state which was a perfect melding of man-made facilities and Mother Nature.

"We kayaked, swam and ate wonderfully prepared traditional meals.

"We luxuriated in our surroundings, away from issues, some of which are contrived to hurt and destroy people.

"It's funny that the wilds of Mother Nature, with its creeks, bays and plant life, seem more orderly than the supposed sophistication of the intelligentsia who claim to know what's best for the social order.

"Sometimes, to see things more clearly, it's incumbent to get away from your surroundings and find different perspectives.

"I have and it's done me a world of good. Give it a try and let me know your feelings."

Myra stopped reading and I complimented her on what she had read. Then we made plans for the weekend.

* * *

As we sat in a Greek restaurant, enjoying our date, Myra said to me, alluding to my just-published book, "You know the knife throwers will be out for you."

"They would come after me if they just found out I gave a contribution to the American Cancer Society because in their eyes I'm the image of evil. It's the old story: Hate the image and ignore the facts, and, My Dear, that has become the mantra of a lot of people in your profession, the journalists, the supposed watchdogs of the people's interest."

Myra picked up her menu, pretending to ignore my diatribe.

Seeing I had made her feel uncomfortable, I said "I didn't mean to upset you. I apologize for my outburst."

"You don't have to apologize. Surely, some members of the traditional media will defend you."

"Why should they? If you stand in the way of a hurricane, you will be destroyed. It's better to run with the pack and receive accolades that you're a member of a noble cause."

"Suppose I take it upon myself to defend you."

"I won't let you do that."

"Why?"

"Because you'll be placing your career and livelihood in jeopardy. I'm used to nonsense. I don't want to see you get destroyed."

"I'm in a profession that exists on the basis of free speech and freedom of the press."

"The trouble with such high-minded terms is: Who is defining them and how are they being defined."

"We're all not evil."

"I didn't say you were. It's only that some people who know better will be cowed into silence."

"Well I'm not one!"

"I wish you would be!"

"And you're the one who castigates my profession as a bunch of hypocrites."

"It's deeper than that."

"Why?"

"I don't want to see my lover get hurt, especially for my sake."

Following that snippet of conversation, we silently contemplated each other's words. Then the conversation lightened as we awaited my inevitable castigation.

CHAPTER XIV

The Mob and Me

My book release was scheduled at an auxiliary auditorium at the college at which I taught. As I was about to enter the facility, I saw scruffy-faced, shabbily clad protestors carrying placards which read: "Boycott Kaplan Who Is Against The Minimum Wage" and "Self-Interest Is Not A Means Of Solving Social Problems. We Must All Work Together." I was approached by an attractively coiffed female TV reporter who, as the saying goes, wanted the camera to love her.

"Dr. Kaplan," she asked, "what is your reaction to the protestors?" As she was asking the question, Myra came upon us.

"My guess is that the majority are unfamiliar with my work. I guess protesting me has become an in thing. It is, as Shakespeare has written, *Much Ado About Nothing*."

"Then what would you tell the protestors?"

"The same thing I'm about to tell you."

"Which is?"

"Read my work so you're able to speak to me on an intelligent level. Just because someone in front of you is carrying a sign doesn't mean you have to follow. I suppose Shakespeare was right after all."

"How so?"

"He wrote: 'All the world is a stage and all the men and women are merely players.'"

"Aren't you being a bit cynical?"

"What do you think?"

"I'm interviewing you."

"Well, I'm asking you."

At that point, the TV reporter, realizing I had probably said all I was going to say, walked away, seemingly discouraged, I assumed.

Anyway, accompanied by Myra, I made my way to the auditorium. As we did, she said, "You could have been a bit more courteous to the TV reporter."

"I simply can't dignify," I replied, "these kinds of settings and these types of people. The whole atmosphere is ludicrous."

"Well," Myra said, "when we get inside the auditorium, things should be more conventional."

I nodded pleasingly as we continued to walk together. Inside was a crowd of conservatively dressed academics and business people awaiting my appearance. This was quite a contrast to the mob scene outside.

I ascended to the podium and began to speak.

"You know," I said, "I respect the right of assemblage and protest. These are pillars of freedom upon which our country is based.

"However, what I've witnessed recently, including what's occurring outside, is that I've been confronted by a mindless mob that is probably unfamiliar with my work.

"With freedom comes responsibility to understand issues. Any fool can follow blindly and if enough fools congregate, you can create frightening distortions.

"My newest book, on the other hand, is a tribute to individualism and freedom, and how these elements have created a better life for mankind by giving us such inventions as cars, computers, electric lights, etc.

"In the main, I condemn the mindlessness of the mob and respect the rights of the individual. May we never be subjected to mob rule."

Then I proceeded to discuss elements of my book.

When I finished, Myra said, "I thought you handled yourself beautifully in the way you castigated the mob and how you discussed your book."

"Really," I replied, "the book contains no earth-shaking revelations. It is a compilation of how individualism and freedom have created a better life for mankind, as a result of entrepreneurs who were motivated by self-interest and profit. It's no more complicated than that."

"Anyway I will defend your cause."

"I wish you would stay out of it."

"Why?"

"Because if I go down, you may be coming with me."

"I think you're being overly concerned and totally naïve."

"I hope you're right."

CHAPTER XV

The Bullseye on My Back

Following the release of my book, *The Individual and the Economy*, I received strong reviews from the financial press which praised my research and writing. On the other hand, *The Sentinel*, the paper at which Myra worked, excoriated the book as an attempt "to criticize national planning as a means to castigate the democratic process."

I laughed when I read that and felt the reviewer had no basic understanding of economic and business history.

In contrast to that review, Myra, in her column, praised the book and lashed out at "the mindless protest movement" which dogged me. She went on to write: "Society will rue the day when it gives into the whims of the mob." She concluded her column by writing, "An elephant can be trained to grab the tail of the elephant in front of him and parade with the rest of the pachyderms in a circle. People, as it relates to the work of Dr. Stephen Kaplan, should know better and rely on their intellect to assess his work and not be part of the elephant parade."

When I read what she had written, I called her, laughing, and thanked her for her support. Then we made plans to have lunch together.

As we sat in the restaurant, Myra asked me if I would be interested in doing some op-ed pieces in contrast to some of the reviews and editorials that have appeared.

"I don't think so," I said. "To do so would, in my opinion, only incite the critics to continue their diatribes against me. You know, Joseph Goebbels, the Nazi propaganda minister, said, 'If you repeat a lie long enough, it becomes the truth.' Certainly, I'm not immune from such outrageous activities."

"As a Jew, grotesquely aware of history, I sympathize with such a point. ... So what is your next step?" Myra asked.

"To continue to be who I am and let the fools be who they are. You can't educate people who are immune to logic."

"I suppose you believe those to be the readers and writers of the *Sentinel*."

"You said that, I didn't."

Myra paused to gather her thoughts and said, "I guess you don't have any more books in the offing."

"Not immediately, but likely I'll be ready with something in a couple of years."

"Do you have a topic?"

"Perhaps I'll do something on the major economists who shaped economic thought, and apply their rationale to the problems of today."

"How do you think that you'll be received by your critics?"

"Since I'm the target of many, not necessarily well. To them, it's not what I write that's important, it's who I am. I figuratively have a bullseye on my back. You know if I were giving away dollar bills on the corner, my critics would find fault."

"You do have an interesting way of putting things."

"Can you think of a better way?"

"Not at the moment," Myra said, smiling.

"I hope one day I can smile a little about this too."

"You will, My Dear. You will."

"I hope if that's the case, we'll be together."

Myra stirred uneasily and said, "Uh, it's getting late. I must get back to the office."

"Let me walk you to your car."

"Thank you," she said.

CHAPTER XVI

Big Government and "Big" Education: The Unholy Alliance

Several months later, Alfred T. Drake, Ph.D., the chancellor at the school at which I worked, received a call from Lieutenant Governor Bradley M. Stevenson and a meeting was set at the state capital.

As Dr. Drake sat with the Lieutenant Governor in his office, the two exchanged pleasantries. Then Mr. Stevenson said, "Let's get down to brass tacks."

"Certainly," Dr. Drake replied.

"You're aware that the amount of the state's appropriation for your university will be coming up in this year's legislative session?"

"Of course," Dr. Drake replied, "and I might add the state has been most generous with its recent appropriations, permitting the school to achieve growth it would not have been able to accomplish otherwise. ... So what seems to be the problem?"

Professor Stephen Kaplan, because of his past testimony before the legislature and due to his writing, has fallen into disfavor with numerous elected officials. As a result, there is a movement to severely curtail or eliminate the appropriation."

"If the appropriation is eliminated, that would be devastating to the school."

"And if Professor Kaplan is unchecked, it could impact the legislative agenda we are pursuing."

"How so?"

"As you know, Professor Kaplan is against raising the minimum wage and for free trade."

"Yes, he's made that a pillar of his writing. ... So what's the problem?"

"Since we are courting labor's vote and need to have protection for certain large industries in our state which have suffered from foreign competition, we can't have him railing against things we hold dear and possibly influencing legislation."

"But, Mr. Stevenson, we believe in academic freedom and this university doesn't muzzle its professors, especially one as distinguished as Dr. Kaplan."

"Then you'll be risking your appropriation because of legislative backlash. While I wholeheartedly support academic freedom and freedom of expression, sometimes you have to be practical about such things."

"Mr. Stevenson, your suggested course of action could create a real dilemma for the university."

"I suppose if it could be arranged to look as if Dr. Kaplan left on his own and the matter were handled discreetly, you can avoid damage and receive a substantial state-funded appropriation."

"Eventually, it is likely the reason for Dr. Kaplan's forced departure will leak out. Then the university will face criticism, and possible sanctions and lawsuits from groups that don't share your agenda, but support the rights of the victim."

"I feel if the matter is handled properly, such problems can be avoided."

"We live in a media-centric age where news and opinions travel at the speed of light. Uh, do you know what a secret is?"

"What?"

"Something that everyone knows."

"Dr. Drake, please understand we will soon need to know your course of action. Good day."

A few days later, Dr. Drake and the president of the school, Pierpont S. Tudor, were discussing my future.

A month later, I was called in to meet the pair and discuss what I thought would be a conference on my succeeding the soon-to-retire Rynard Flemming as head of the university's Department of Economics, making me one of the youngest academics in the country to hold such a position. I felt if I could ascend to such a role, this would be quite a feather in my cap and a validation of my views, research and writing. As I sat in a comfortable leather chair next to Dr. Drake, President Tudor said, "There is no easy way for me to put this, so I might as well just come out and say it."

When I heard that, I froze with anxiety.

"Dr. Kaplan," he said, "I believe it would be in everyone's best interest if you would leave this university."

"Why?" I asked, stunned.

"I'm going to depend on your integrity to completely keep what I'm about to say in the strictest of confidence so we can proceed to reach an acceptable monetary settlement."

"I'm listening," I said.

"Because of your views, we're being threatened with a curtailment or elimination of state funds, which we desperately need."

"What happened to the academic freedom this university promises?"

"To be perfectly blunt, I'm afraid money trumps that mission."

"So I might be asked to take taxpayer money as a settlement to leave this university."

Dr. Drake nodded.

"And," I replied, "they call me a Neanderthal for my views, and they wonder why I continually rail against the foolish expenditure of public funds."

"Look," said President Tudor, "we're aware you're a tenured professor, so the settlement we will likely propose would be rather generous."

"I'll listen and in all probability will go along and remain silent about the departure I'm *forced* to make."

"Good," said President Tudor.

"However," I said, "the trouble with secrets is that sooner or later everybody learns about them. That's when life becomes interesting."

I then said good-bye and waited to hear the terms of the proposed settlement, because I knew I could never be where I wasn't wanted.

CHAPTER XVII

My Defender Wouldn't Listen

I was soon on the phone with Myra.

"You sound kind of depressed," she said.

"Oh, it's nothing," I replied.

"Come on, I know you well enough to realize when something is bothering you. Now tell me what it is."

"It's nothing, really."

"Stephen …"

"Okay, okay. It's highly likely I'll soon be leaving the university."

"What? … How did this come about?"

"Oh, it's something I've been considering for quite sometime."

"Stephen …"

"What is it?"

"I know you're not being truthful with me. Now tell me what's really going on."

"I told you."

"My journalistic instincts tell me otherwise, and I may wish to pursue the reason why a distinguished scholar such as yourself is *suddenly* leaving."

"I would appreciate it if you would not get involved."

"Why?"

"Because certain forces may become arrayed against you, and you'll perish as a result."

"I'm in a profession that prides itself on ferreting out the truth and supporting the public's right to know."

"Don't be naïve. Some things aren't meant for the public to know."

"I'll be the judge of that."

"If you get involved, I may never speak to you again."

"Why?"

"Because you're going to get hurt for my sake, and I don't wish to be party to that."

"It's okay for you to stand up for your beliefs. Why can't I?"

"Because I'm not worth you throwing your career away."

"It sounds to me like you're being forced out."

"Stay out of it, dammit," I ordered.

"I'll be the judge of when or if that's appropriate."

"I wish you would take my advice."

Soon, I worked out a settlement with the college, but Myra wouldn't listen to me.

She began to do multiple interviews with anonymous sources who gave her information. Then she did a column. It read, in part, "Dr. Stephen Kaplan has been forced out of a university professorship because he believed in academic freedom.

"Due to his belief that he had license to write and speak based on sound research, he ran afoul of forces in the state legislature who threatened the school with its appropriation if he were to remain. As a result, Dr. Kaplan, who was the likely choice to head the university's Department of Economics when that position opens, is now an unemployed professor, with a substantial record of publishing that has been positively reviewed by academics in his field.

"Has his former university become an institution where seamy politics has trumped the process of education and freedom of speech?

"It certainly seems so."

Myra's column was quickly brought to my attention, and after I read it, I called her.

"Why did you get involved?" I asked.

"Because I hate to see injustice and someone has to take a position that certain behavior can't be tolerated."

"You don't understand," I said.

"Understand what?" she asked.

"They'll be coming after you next."

CHAPTER XVIII

Myra's Destiny

Myra was soon called to meet with Stewart Townsend, the managing editor of the *Sentinel*.

"Ms. Foreman," the managing editor said, "it has been brought to my attention that you have a romantic relationship with Dr. Stephen Kaplan, whom you've written about often."

"That's correct and I've mentioned that in my columns."

"As you know we have a rule against covering people you share intimacy with."

"If I might say so, that's the most-abused rule there is around here. After all, it is well known that you dated your future wife, Susan Strom, when she headed a local chapter of the National Organization for Women, while you were covering her group."

"Excuse me, Ms. Foreman, this is about you, not me."

"I'm sorry, I didn't mean to interrupt you."

"Ms. Foreman, you have left me with no other choice."

"Oh," Myra said squeamishly.

"You no longer work for the *Sentinel*. You have three days to remove your belongings. Helene Bishop will be taking over your column."

Immediately following her meeting, Myra called to tell me the news.

I said to her, "I told you not to get involved."

"Can't you be more sympathetic!" she said.

"I'm sorry, I didn't mean to be so abrupt. … Uh, would you like some company?"

"Sure, come to my apartment as soon as possible."

I went and never saw her so distraught. As I tried to comfort her, she said, "Here I thought I was doing something noble and, as a result, I've been terminated. I should have learned to shill like the rest of the bastards for those who are in favor and castigate those on the outs. It's a big game played by egregious conformists who think they are otherwise."

"Yes and those 'egregious conformists' call me the misfit."

"I've come to learn that words can have no meaning."

"Except when you cross the line," I interrupted.

"I make my living with words and have learned the hard way what you have just meant, though I was blind not to have realized it long before."

"I suppose we all learn the hard way what we thought what was cast in stone has the strength of tissue paper."

"The trouble is," Myra said, "is what we're talking about can't be found in too many books."

"As the saying goes, 'If you wish to learn, don't go to school.' … Anyway, tomorrow is another day and we'll go on."

"Yeah," Myra said, "we'll go on because we must."

"Yes, we must," I affirmed. ... "Uh, are you up to doing anything now?"

"No, but stay with me a little while longer. Then I want to be alone to gather my thoughts. After that, I'll go to bed early."

"Okay, but I'll call you early tomorrow."

Myra nodded affirmatively.

I soon kissed her good night and left.

I called her the next day and asked, "How are you feeling?"

"I'm feeling better. A good night's sleep will do that."

"I know," I said. "Without a regular schedule, I've had plenty of time to practice lying down."

"Uh, I wish I could laugh at that."

"I'm sorry, I didn't mean to upset you."

After a pause, I asked, "Have you thought about your immediate plans?"

"I'm thinking of going away for awhile, possibly to Europe."

"I'd like to go with you."

"I may wish to travel alone."

"Whatever you wish," I said. ... "How about if we have lunch together today?"

"I'll call you later and let you know."

CHAPTER XIX

Love Is Where You Find It

Myra, in an effort to escape her surroundings, hurriedly prepared a trip to Europe, and began to ignore my frequent phone calls, e-mails and impromptu visits to her residence. As a result, I assumed our relationship was over, which saddened me deeply.

Meanwhile, my job hunting was not going very well, and I was wondering, in spite of my record of academic achievement, if I had been blacklisted by the university community. Needless to say, my life had become something of a wreck. One day I received a letter in the mail from The New Liberty Foundation, a conservative think tank, which outlined a position that it was creating for a "writer and thinker who espouses traditional economic philosophy and libertarian views."

"My God," I thought to myself, "this would be perfect for me, and I wouldn't have to be at the mercy of a university that was dependent on government funds, where I could be singled out because of my intellectual leanings and forced to leave."

After several phone calls to discuss the position, I was invited to New York to be interviewed by P. Forest Whitaker, the head of the foundation.

On a Tuesday morning, I boarded a bus and saw Myra sitting in the rear of the vehicle.

I approached her and asked, "Is the seat taken next to you?"

"I think so because when I purchased my ticket I was told the bus was now sold-out."

"If I could persuade the seat-holder next to you to move, would you mind?"

"Not at all."

A few minutes later, a young woman sat next to Myra. I asked her if she wouldn't mind taking my seat so I "could sit next to an old acquaintance?"

"I'm alone," she said, "so it doesn't matter."

"It's not good to be alone," I responded. The woman looked at me quizzically and left her seat as Myra smiled.

"It's wonderful to see you again. You're looking more attractive than ever."

"Thank you," she replied, "and you're looking quite well, too. … By the way, what's bringing you to New York?"

"I'm being interviewed for a position at a conservative think tank."

"So you're leaving university life?"

"Well, the better answer is a misfit like me may have been blacklisted, so I have no choice. Besides, the position I'm about to be offered sounds perfect for me, and might include a weekly column which may be syndicated."

"So the 'misfit' rises."

"Hopefully," I laughed, "and, by the way, what is bringing you to Gotham?"

"*The New York Horizon* is looking for a columnist who can supply fresh commentary on a variety of subjects ranging from weighty issues to the social scene."

"If you get the position, must you conform to the norms of the paper, or, if you deviate, will you be riding another bus?"

"I thought part of being a conformist in the newspaper business was you were allowed to express yourself freely. I should have known better. If I had, I wouldn't be sitting next to you."

"Well, that's not so bad, I'd like to think."

"No, it's not," Myra replied.

"Anyway, I believed in academic freedom and I'm on the same bus you're on."

"I've noticed," Myra laughed.

"I suppose in life you have to know when to be a conformist and when to be a misfit. You have to pick your spots."

"In spite of what I was educated to believe, I know you're right."

"The one thing I know is that we can be right for one another," I said, unhesitantly. "By the way, this misfit wants to know if you're free this evening for some fine dining and dancing?"

"On such short notice?"

"Yes …"

"Oh, of course I am."

I took Myra's hand and began to kiss her passionately.

After we finished, she said, "Why do I have to love a misfit?"

"For the same reason I love you."

"Which is?"

"Who knows!"

About the Author

Mark Carp is the author of *The Columnist* and *The Conformist and the Misfit*, two novellas. He has written six novels: *Mr. Show Business, Segalvitz, Abraham: The Last Jew, The Extraordinary Times of Ordinary People, The End of Hell*, and *Naomi's "American" Family*. He has also written *Cain, Abel and the Family Cohen*, a fictional memoir. Mr. Carp lives in Baltimore, Maryland, and holds a BS degree from the University of Maryland and an MS degree from The Johns Hopkins University.